Blood and Water

Also by Peter de Polnay

Fiction

SPRING SNOW AND ALGY

PETER DE POLNAY

Blood and Water

St. Martin's Press   New York

Library of Congress Cataloging in Publication Data

De Polnay, Peter, 1906-
    Blood and water.

    I. Title.
PZ3.D4407Bl3   [PR6007.E635]   823'.9'12   75-40784

Blood and Water

I

A loud thud awoke Claud who in his dream had been standing on a windowledge, ready to hurl himself into a torrent
that rushed past the house. He blinked, then laughed silently.
Wilf, his golden retriever, had fallen out of the armchair, as
often happened when the fat dog was chasing rabbits in his
sleep. 'Get back on the chair,' Claud mumbled, but Wilf
preferred to stay where he had dropped. As he was about to
turn on his side, Claud remembered his father complaining
after dinner of a pain in his chest. He got out of bed, went
barefoot into the passage, switched on the light, and tiptoed
to his father's bedroom door, which he opened soundlessly.

The full moon shone into the vast room, picking out every
object. In the large bed lay Mr Darnell on his back, his eyes
open, his still dark hair the shape of a halo on the pillow.
Claud held his breath, waiting for his father to speak to him.
I wanted to see if you were all right, he prepared to say in
case his father remonstrated with him for the intrusion. Mr
Darnell said nothing, which was strange, since his open eyes
meant that he wasn't asleep. Wilf had followed Claud to the
door, pushed past him and trotted up to the bed. Claud feared
to call him back because of the noise his words would make.
Wilf raised his paws, and was beginning to climb on the bed.
'Down,' said Claud loudly, waiting for his father to ask him
what the hell he and Wilf were doing in his bedroom. His
father remained silent. Wilf got off the bed, and with his tail
drawn in, cringed his way out of the bedroom. What was
wrong with the dog? Claud went up to the bed, his heart
beating fast.

'Father,' he said. 'Anything wrong, father?'

Mr Darnell's eyes were normally full of expression, and when he smiled they smiled with him. Now they were staring past Claud with no message in them. 'Father,' cried Claud, and, something he wouldn't dare have done even a few seconds before, he shook him by the shoulder. The eyes didn't waver, but the mouth opened. 'My father is dead,' said Claud, as though addressing a crowd awaiting the news. He shook his head because he couldn't believe his own words. 'Speak to me,' he said, though nothing would have frightened him more than the dead man speaking to him. The marble wall that separates the living from the dead had risen already. 'I refuse to believe it, father,' he said, though he knew it for a fact.

He sat down on the bed, took his father's hand, and held it in a tight grip. It wasn't yet cold. What am I to do? he asked himself. Should I wake up Lil? What good could Lil do? She would start howling, which wouldn't help. He wished his father could tell him what to do in the circumstances. His father had had an answer to everything, was never perplexed, and took all in his stride. It struck Claud like a stab that he could rely on his father no more. He thought he would faint, so held on hard to the dead man's hand. He didn't faint, in fact he had a strong urge to smoke a cigarette. He fought it down.

When Claud was fifteen, his father, in the course of one of their long, delightful chats observed that he would die first if Nature stuck to its rules. 'I want to die first,' said Claud. 'I don't want to live without you.'

'You want to force me to live without you,' Mr Darnell smiled. 'You're unkind, Claud.'

That was seven years ago, and remembering his father's words, Claud's eyes filled with tears. 'Oh, father,' he mumbled. He ought to call Lil, but why should he? He wanted to stay alone with his father.

The moon went behind a cloud, and the room became pitch dark. Instinctively, Claud switched on the bedside lamp, which lit up the dead man's face. He looked so composed, Claud thought. He bent forward, and their chins nearly touched. Mr Darnell had been a strikingly handsome man with regular features and a fine moustache. Death had not altered that remarkable face. He looked satisfied with himself and the unseen world around him. Why can't the dead come back? It was only a matter of hours since he had been alive. If the clock were put back, say, four hours, he could still talk to him. The whole business was ridiculous if you examined it dispassionately. Four hours ago his father had said he was going to London for the day.

'When will you be back?'

'Before dinner.'

It was too ridiculous. He should say to him, 'Snap out of it, father. You know you must go to London for the day.' He went on staring at the dead man, and the longer he stared the less he believed that his father could be dead, the creeping pallor notwithstanding. You live with a person for twenty-two years, he is in your mind all the time, your thoughts and actions are entwined with his : you can't admit or realise that his influence has gone without him giving you any warning. His father should have warned him that after tonight nothing would be the same again. His father's wrist-watch said it was ten past five : it was remiss of him not to have told him when they separated after dinner that he would be dead before morning. In the distance a cock crowed.

'You can't do this to me, father,' Claud said, choking.

Mr Darnell's chin sagged as if it wanted to drop off all on its own. Claud had seen him now and then falling asleep in the sitting-room after a meal, his mouth open, snoring lightly. He shook his head because no snore would escape that open mouth. Another cock crowed, then a third, and the May dawn was in the offing. Sooner or later he must call Lil. He took the packet of cigarettes from the bedside table. There were only five in it. He looked at his father as though asking his permission to smoke, then lit up.

'I don't believe it,' he said in a loud voice.

To evoke his own short past seemed impossible with his father gone; to envisage the future without him was even more impossible. He saw himself on a perch from which he couldn't descend, having no idea how he had got on it. When

9

he had smoked half the cigarette, he took it to his room to stub it out because his father detested seeing cigarette stubs in the ashtray.

Wilf lay in his armchair, and feebly wagged his tail. 'You're not a very faithful dog,' said Claud, patting his large head. He went to the window, Wilf following, and he leaned out, remembering the torrent he had seen in his dream. He had read somewhere that you find nothing in your dreams that you haven't seen in one form or another with your own eyes. He must have seen that fast-running water in a picture or in the cinema; nonetheless it was strange since he couldn't imagine a torrent sweeping through the peaceful garden under the window. Had his father sent it to announce his death? He should go back to him.

On reaching the dead man's bedroom it struck him that if he continued to shunt between their bedrooms the present situation would become endless; and he saw himself alone in the world going from one room to another with nobody to speak to. He climbed up to the second floor to call Lil.

2

Lil slept badly at night. In the daytime she was willing to fall asleep anywhere and in any position, but when night came she was cursed by wakefulness. She had a television set, which she could look at from the bed, books were piled high on the bed-side table, and on another table were a loaf of bread, some sliced ham, butter, two plates and a bottle of stout in case she felt peckish. This she seldom did, so in the morning she would take it all down, the bread and the ham dry, the butter runny. She was lying on her back reading a book she could make no sense of, yet convinced she had read it before.

Though she carried little fat she was a large woman, because of her bone structure. Her eyes were alarmingly blue, and her pointed chin suggested lack of determination. She had masses of fair hair, and her body was swan-white. She had to keep herself continuously occupied, since she had no gift for amusing herself. Her own thoughts and images were incapable of keeping her company, so she had to read, look, talk, listen, bustle, use her hands. In brief, it was unthinkable for her to be on her own. She would carry her transistor from one room to another, would pick up a two-days-old newspaper and gaze at it avidly rather than sit with her hands in her lap.

'Who's that?' she called on hearing a loud knock at her door. Naturally, she was expecting Mr Darnell to answer.

'Lil,' said Claud's voice, 'an awful thing has happened. Come at once.'

'What are you up to?' she said gruffly, jumping out of bed.

She invariably slept in red pyjamas, this being her favourite colour, and without bothering to put on her dressing gown she burst into the passage. Claud blinked at the sight of so much red. 'Come with me,' he said, and preceded her to the bedroom. Dawn had come in through the window, and the bedside lamp lit up the dead man's face. 'Oh, my God,' she exclaimed, then, throwing herself on the bed, she shouted, 'Snap out of it.'

Claud stared at her aghast, for in his presence Lil had invariably been deferential to his father. His eyes nearly popped out as she sat down on the bed and pulled his father's head on to her lap. The pallor of death became more conspicuous with the head resting against the red pyjamas. She burst into tears, her hair almost covering her face, and said to the dead man, ignoring the son, 'I expected it.'

'Why?' Claud couldn't help asking.

'Because I loved him,' she muttered.

Claud didn't know what to say. With those words she had broken the unwritten contract between her, the father and the son. She had come to the house as cook-housekeeper; Claud's mother lived in France. Lil ran the house alone, and when there was no guest she took her meals with them. 'We live in a democratic age,' was the explanation his father gave. Never a word or gesture betrayed their real relationship. After lunch as well as after dinner she withdrew to her territory which consisted of the kitchen on the ground floor and her bedroom on the second. Thus Mr Darnell had no reason to suppose his son would guess her position in his life. As a matter of fact, faithful Claud guessed nothing. It was Ludmilla who had assured him that Lil was her master's mistress, and loyally he refused to believe her. He bowed his head, because now he had to. On the rare occasions his mother had come over she and Lil appeared to get on fine. Would they now, with him gone? It was the first time he had thought of his mother since he discovered that his father had died while he slept.

Lil closed the dead man's eyes, then told Claud to fetch a handkerchief, a large one, out of the third drawer from the top in the chest of drawers. Claud thought she needed it for her tears, and was astonished when she used it to tie his father's chin. She laid the head back on the pillow, stood up and stretched her arms. The pyjama coat being unbuttoned, he saw her big breasts and rosy nipples. Blushing, he turned his head away.

'Go and ring Dr Corry,' she said.

'He'll be in bed, Lil.'

'Who cares? He must come at once.'

He turned back from the door : Lil had sat down on the bed again, her white breasts showing, tears coursing down her cheeks. His father was dead, Lil had been his mistress, and he had seen her breasts.

'He's coming,' he called from the passage on his way back from the telephone. Because of the breasts he didn't want to enter the room, but as there was no answer he peeped in : his father was alone, and with the handkerchief tied round his face he looked as though he had toothache. Where had Lil gone? For a moment he feared that she had gone to kill herself : she loved his father who probably had loved her, too, and she wanted to go after him. There were two shotguns and a rook rifle in a cupboard downstairs in the study. He waited for the shot, wondering what to do if she really did away with herself. Lay her out beside his father? He shook his head, since that was the last thing a decorous man like his father would tolerate, even in death. Was one so very decorous if one had a mistress? Lil appeared, dressed, and he couldn't resist glancing at her bosom. Dress and bra covered it.

'Dr Corry is coming,' Claud said.

'Open the other window, too. Where's Wilf?'

'He came in with me, but when he saw father was dead he escaped. Lil, I just can't believe it.'

'What?'

'Father being dead.'

She shrugged her shoulders, and then said, 'Go and dress.'

Claud was dressed and back in the bedroom when Dr Corry rang the front door bell. Barking furiously, Wilf chased down the stairs.

'I'd bark, too, if I could,' muttered Lil. Claud followed Wilf to let the doctor in.

'Are you sure?' asked the doctor.

Claud nodded emphatically, the doctor went up the stairs, and he remained in the doorway. Let Lil deal with him. He preferred gazing at the garden on which his father wouldn't set eyes again. The garden was mostly lawn and shrubs. Beyond it extended the fields, and the view ended with the farm buildings and sheds. A depressing landscape, especially in winter. Yet Claud loved it because it represented his past, present and future. He had lived in the house since he could remember, and, in accordance with his father's wish, he would farm the land after Ringham, the farm manager, retired. 'I don't want you to take part in the hustle and bustle of modern life,' his father had said. 'The farm will cater for most of your needs, and working and living here your existence will be serene and harmonious.' Ringham, thought Mr Darnell, could teach him all he needed to know about farming. Claud accepted whatever his father said as Gospel truth and so, when the headmaster at his school shook his head sadly because he wouldn't go to University, Claud simply pointed out that it was contrary to his father's intention. Now, with his father dead, it was doubly his duty to go along the road Mr Darnell had traced for him.

In the distance King, the cowman, was crossing the field on his way to the cowshed. On most days Claud would join him and Ringham, and Bert, who drove the tractor, would also appear. Then the three of them would keep themselves busy, chatting with Claud and answering his questions. Thus at lunch Claud could answer his father's.

He went in to the passage leading to the kitchen for his gum boots. The pair his father wore was next to them. He called Wilf, and they started for the sheds. Ringham saw him, and came slowly towards him. In dark moments of doubt Claud thought that Ringham was entirely bogus, and that his act of the staunch husbandman was put on for his father's benefit. However, such moments were rare.

'My father is dead,' cried Claud.

'What do you say?' shouted Ringham.

'My father died in the night.'

Ringham's red cheeks turned pale, for the young man's loss might also mean the loss of his job. With Darnell he knew where he stood; with the young you never did. 'This is the most terrible news I ever heard, Mr Claud,' he said. 'It sure breaks my heart. But how did it happen?' Claud explained, and while he spoke Ringham stroked his toothbrush moustache, as ginger coloured as his hair, searching hard for the appropriate words.

'But he wasn't old,' he said.

'Fifty-two.'

'Was in such good health.'

'There you are.'

'Such a loss for all of us, Mr Claud, and for you it must be something terrible.' Claud nodded, and Ringham's eyes shone, for he had found the right words.

'The king is dead, long live the king. Count on me, Mr Claud, like Mr Darnell could count on me.' He held out his hand which Claud shook, embarrassed, muttering his thanks. The doctor, he saw, had left the house accompanied by Lil. After the doctor had driven away he said he had better go in, and with Wilf at his heel he hurried back. He turned his head once : Ringham was talking to Bert and King. He sighed. The more people who knew about it, the more irrevocable his father's death appeared.

'Come to the kitchen,' said Lil, who was still on the door-step. 'I'm not laying the table in the dining-room.'

'What did the doctor say?'

'What did you expect him to say?' she grunted. 'We'll have coffee. Has more kick than tea.'

Claud sat down at the long kitchen table, nodding once or twice. His father was definitely dead since, if he were alive, his son wouldn't be sitting at the kitchen table. He looked up as he heard the sound of bacon frying. 'I don't want breakfast, Lil. Couldn't swallow a thing.'

'You bloody well have to,' she said without turning round. 'Starving yourself won't bring him back. If it could I wouldn't ever eat again this side of the grave.'

'I'm going to call Father Turle.'

'That's your department,' said Lil.

'Anyway, on Sunday we went both to confession and communion, so he died practically without a sin.' Lil pretended not to hear him. 'Still, he must have absolution.'

'You eat this,' said Lil, putting a plate of bacon and eggs in front of him. 'I'll be having the same.'

Bringing her cup and plate to the table she sat down beside him. He blushed at her nearness, remembering the ample white breasts and rosy nipples.

'After you've phoned the priest,' said Lil, speaking with her mouth full, 'ring up your mother. She'll want to come to the funeral.'

'You ring her, Lil.'

'You're the son.'

'I wouldn't know what to say to her.' He couldn't explain to Lil, who wouldn't understand, that he feared his mother because he hardly knew her. The yearly visits she paid to the house dug deeper the ditch that separated them.

'All right,' said Lil, 'I'll ring her.'

'It's such a help having you here. If you weren't here I'd lose my head.'

'Well, don't. I won't remain here long.'

'What do you mean?' he asked, frightened.

'What I said. Your father's dead, so my life here is dead, too. You're old enough to look after yourself. Anyway, you'll marry Ludmilla Coke, so you've no cause to worry.'

'I'm not sure she wants to marry me.'

'I am.'

'Even so, what am I to do with this house without you?'

'Sell it, Claud, sell the farm too.'

'Never,' he exclaimed. 'I owe it to my father to stay here and farm.'

'We owe the dead tears, but not obedience. Listen to me, boy. I know what I'm talking about. You won't ever make a farmer, Claud. It isn't in you.'

'Have you said that to father?'

'I never told him anything. It wasn't part of our bargain. But with him gone I can tell you. Sell the farm, sell the house and . . .'

' . . . do what?'

'That'll be for you to decide,' she said, lighting a cigarette. She poured out more coffee. 'I don't want to go away from here thinking you're making a mess of your life, doing what you don't really like doing.' Her blue eyes were on him, hard and unflinching. 'Most people do what they don't like doing. Why should you, too?'

'I was brought up to it.'

'He got it into his head that the ideal life is a quiet life, and nothing is more quiet than country life. But we're talking of your life, and I don't see why at twenty-two you should resign yourself to a quiet life.'

'What do you want me to do? Become a soldier or a fireman?'

'I'm not joking, Claud.'

'Father was a soldier, and that wasn't a joke.'

'It wasn't,' she said drily.

'DSO, MC, not bad.'

'He chucked it after the war. And there's no war now, so think of something more up to date.'

'I could never go against his wish,' said Claud. 'I'll stay here, but you must stay, too.'

'I've told you I won't. Once everything is settled I'll pull out.'

'How old are you, Lil?'

'Thirty-seven, but what has that to do with it?'

'Of course, you could marry.'

'No man could mean anything to me after him.'

'So you loved father.'

'No bloody business of yours,' she said, rising from the table. 'Go and phone your priest, then I'll ring your mother.'

The study was small, the window large, and as Claud sat down at the table he saw Jones and Mrs Jones entering the garden, he the gardener-handyman, she the daily woman, both in their late forties. Jones moved as though afraid of collapsing, she like a duck. Claud frowned at the telephone. If Lil was his father's mistress, his father had lived in perpetual sin. She couldn't have been, in fact it was out of the question, for hadn't his father been to communion yesterday? Perhaps she had been many years ago. If you live with a woman who isn't your wife, no priest can absolve you. He must have got it all wrong, his father was above that sort of thing, not one to have an affair with his housekeeper, too much of a man of honour for that. Hadn't Ludmilla's mother said repeatedly, 'Your father looks like the perfect Edwardian grand seigneur?' He got up and went to the kitchen.

Lil was talking to the Joneses. Having put a scarf round her head, she looked as she had done every morning, the cook-housekeeper getting ready for her daily work. He beckoned to her and she came out into the passage. The Joneses had their backs to him, and thus they couldn't see him. 'What is it now?' Lil asked.

'What am I to say to Father Turle?'

'Told you it's your business.'

'I mean what did Dr Corry say? What did father die of?'

'Heart stopped beating. He'd a weak heart. Doctor said he wasn't surprised.'

'We were, and I bet father was too.'

'Go and phone,' she said with a catch in her voice.

She put on a white overall, then went upstairs. A few minutes later Claud joined her. 'He's coming,' he said. 'He asked what arrangements I'd made about the funeral. I told him I hadn't thought about it, so he said he'd send the undertaker round.' They were outside his father's bedroom.

'You'll have to deal with the undertaker, Claud. I'm going out.'

'Where?'

'To get food for the day. But first I'll ring your mother.'

He went downstairs with her, was stopped by the Joneses who said they were ever so sorry and they just couldn't believe it. Then they went up to have a look at the dead man, while he remained near the study, not to listen but to wait for Lil to come out. 'Is that you, Margery?' he heard Lil's voice ask, and he blushed because in his presence she always addressed his mother as Mrs Darnell. He hurried to the sitting-room, which his father had referred to as the library on account of the two book cases. 'Your mother is flying over today, she'll be here tonight,' said Lil from the door. 'I'm going out now. You ought to ring Mr Viner, the solicitor.'

'Mother will do that.'

'You have to, you're the heir.'

He watched her taking the car from the garage, then driving off. Father Turle arrived a few minutes later. Strange, Claud reflected, that Lil was never around when the priest came to the house.

3

Mrs Coke and her daughter Ludmilla had finished breakfast in their narrow dining-room, which had a french window giving onto the garden, a fine garden, as Mrs Coke was a keen, knowledgeable gardener. She was in her late forties, with a doll-like face innocent of wrinkles. She had an enchanting smile, and was so proud of it that she smiled all the time. Her husband was counsellor in an embassy to a grim Warsaw Pact country; she and her daughter stayed with him only during winter since she couldn't neglect the garden in other seasons. For her the husband lived in perpetual snow. Ludmilla was taller than her mother, who said that people surely took her daughter to be her sister. Ludmilla didn't mind. In fact, little ruffled her, as she considered life an excuse for being lazy. She spent her days doing absolutely nothing, and was bored only when there was no male in view. She had fair hair and blue eyes. She was twenty-six, four years older than Claud, whom she was determined to marry. She liked his looks, and besides, he lived only two miles away, so once they were married she could commute between the two houses. Driving a car was her sole hobby. She could go out in the car for hours, and if asked on her return where she had been she could truthfully confess she hadn't the vaguest idea.

'What will you do this morning?' Mrs Coke asked.

'I haven't seen the papers yet,' said Ludmilla.

'There isn't much in them.'

'That's what you say,' smiled Ludmilla. 'I always find something that interests me.'

'Are you expecting Claud to come over?'

'He said last night he would . . . What is it, Gretchen?'

Gretchen was the Austrian maid who had been with them for a number of years, fat as a dumpling and a loud and fast talker. Her eyes were shining, her cheeks were flushed. 'Mr Darnell is dead,' she announced.

'What are you talking about?' said Mrs Coke.

'Mr Ringham came to tell me. He died in his sleep. It was Mr Claud who found him dead in his bed. The doctor says heart attack killed him. Mr Ringham doesn't know yet when the burial is. I asked how old he was. Fifty-two. You wouldn't believe to die at fifty-two, and he didn't look ill.'

Ludmilla turned to watch her mother's reaction. Mrs Coke put out her half-smoked, after-breakfast cigarette, then rose from the table. 'How ghastly,' she said.

'I'll ring Claud at once,' said Ludmilla.

'One doesn't ring on such occasions,' said Mrs Coke. 'You write him a letter, take it round and drop it into the letter box.'

'Ridiculous,' said Ludmilla. 'We're too close for letters, he and I.'

'Miss Ludmilla is right,' said Gretchen. 'He will want to see her.'

Mrs Coke sat down again and lit another cigarette. Gretchen remained in the doorway, and as neither mother nor daughter dared send her out the room they began speaking in French, a language Gretchen didn't understand. Tired of the unknown tongue, Gretchen left, banging the door behind her. Mother and daughter reverted to English.

'Looks suspicious to me,' said Mrs Coke. 'He was in perfect health. I shouldn't say it, but don't you think that the house-keeper woman might have poisoned him?'

'What on earth for?'

'Mistresses do poison their lovers from time to time.'

'I don't believe it for a moment,' said Ludmilla. 'With him dead she'll have to go, so it isn't in her interest to kill him.'

'Why should she have to go? He may have left the house to her.'

'He loved Claud too much for that. I never saw a more devoted father in my life. Daddy is a dwarf compared to him.'

'Leave your father out of it,' said Mrs Coke sharply.

'That isn't difficult,' smiled Ludmilla. 'The more I think of it the more ridiculous your idea sounds. We haven't even the right to say she was his mistress. The few times we've been to their house she behaved more discreetly than Gretchen does here. We've no right to say anything against her.'

'Why does the wife live abroad? Because she couldn't put up with her?'

'The last time the wife was back,' said Ludmilla, wondering why she stood up for Lil, whom she couldn't bear, 'I saw the two of them, wife and housekeeper, walking in the garden and chatting like bosom friends.'

'You really saw them?'

'I was driving past.'

'Hold your horses,' said Mrs Coke, getting up. 'Let's see what happens first.'

'What do you mean?'

'You know perfectly well what I mean,' said Mrs Coke with her sweet smile. 'I'll write to Claud after lunch.'

She went out through the french window to tend the herbaceous border. Ludmilla lit a cigarette, and fell into a reverie.

She felt that her mother wasn't keen on her marrying Claud because of the age difference, upon which she never ceased to remark. 'Do you think it'll make much difference to him at seventy, having a wife four years older limping along at his side while he gets about on crutches?' was Ludmilla's reply to that. It was a waste of time and breath to try to explain to her mother her reasons for wanting to marry Claud. She was an only child who since childhood had longed for a brother, and when she met Claud, he aged eleven, she fifteen, she could have wept with joy, for in him she had found the brother she was waiting for, the little brother whom she could cuddle. At the age of twenty she had tried it out with a man of thirty. It was a complete failure, even the memory of it made her sick, so she tried no more, and went on cuddling the little brother, resolved to promote him to husband. That a husband would want from her what the man of thirty had taken didn't enter her calculations. She saw the future as one of holding Claud in her arms and kissing that sweet face of his. The prospect of it made her blissfully happy.

With sudden decision she jumped up from the chair. Hang mother, she would drive over to console her Claud. She heard the door open, turned round, and there was Claud in the doorway.

'Claud,' she cried, 'I know, my poor, darling Claud.'

She threw her arms round him (she was slightly the taller) and held him close. He felt her breasts under the summer dress, and remembered Lil's. 'What can I do to console you, Claud?' she whispered. He had a good mind to ask her to show him her breasts. He knew he wouldn't dare to, and probably they would mean nothing to him.

'It's awful, isn't it?' he said.

'How did he die?'

Claud sat down on the chair Mrs Coke had vacated, then told his woeful tale, starting with Wilf dropping off the chair. 'He must have sensed it,' she said. 'Dogs do.'

'I'm lost,' said Claud. 'You can't understand what our relationship was. He meant everything to me. I loved him, I admired him, was proud of him, and he never let me down.

I'd a friend at school who told me that he had caught his father out in telling a lie, and that it had shattered his faith in him. My father never told a lie.'

'Like George Washington,' said Ludmilla, unable to resist a giggle.

'Don't laugh, I'm telling you the truth. He was above other men.'

'He must have been, because daddy and mother are the worst possible liars.'

'We were too close to each other to need lies or deception.'

'What about Lil the housekeeper? Did he talk to you about her?'

'Lil talked about him this morning.'

'What did she say?' asked Ludmilla eagerly.

'She said that she loved him, but said it so nicely – should I say respectfully – that I realised there couldn't have been anything wrong between them.'

'You don't know much about life, my own Claud, but I like you for that. When is the funeral?'

'On Thursday.'

'We'll go to it. Where?'

'Folkestone.'

'Isn't Dover nearer?'

'Father never liked Dover. He said it reminded him of the two years he was cooped up there during the war.'

Mrs Coke came in through the french window, exclaiming, 'My poor Claud, I can't tell you how sorry I am. Your father was such a handsome man. I'm sure he looks handsome in death too.'

'Very handsome,' said Claud, 'but they're taking him away this afternoon.'

'The way of all flesh,' said Mrs Coke, and Ludmilla turned her head so that her mother shouldn't see the merriment in her eyes. 'Poor Miss Cowling, your housekeeper, must be very upset.'

'She wants to leave,' said Claud.

'Don't stop her,' said Ludmilla, and received a warning glance from her mother.

'I'll miss her terribly,' said Claud. 'Don't know what I'll do without her.'

'Won't your mother come back to live with you?' asked Mrs Coke. Ludmilla frowned.

'The English climate doesn't agree with mother,' said Claud.

'So she chooses to live in the South of France,' said Mrs Coke. 'Lumbago, pleurisy, pneumonia, bronchitis, that's what the South of France stands for. I ought to know. Spent a winter there once. Was ill all the time.'

'Perhaps she likes being ill,' said Ludmilla.

'Mother is never ill,' said Claud. 'I ought to go back, really.'

'I'll see you to the car,' said Ludmilla.

She and Claud walked to the car. 'I'll get in for a moment,' she said. 'I want a kiss.'

He kissed her hard, his tongue trying to force its way into her mouth. 'Don't,' she said, 'I don't like that sort of kiss.' The man she had been to bed with had kissed like that. 'You're above it, my darling Claud.' He touched her breasts. 'Don't,' she said again. 'Put your face against mine, and let's stay like that for a moment.'

While sitting there cheek to cheek he couldn't help asking himself whether marrying Ludmilla would be much fun. Anyway, with his father dead he couldn't marry for a year at least. He stroked Ludmilla's knee, but as his hand started to move up she shook herself free. 'Men are pigs,' she said. 'I don't want you to be one. Come in this evening.'

'I can't, mother is arriving.'

4

Margery Darnell was remarkably tall, a long stork Lil called her in her mind on the rare occasions she thought of her. However, tonight there was no way of ignoring her existence, for the tall, thin woman whose head was too small for her height filled the house with her voice and her continuous rushing from one room to another. At dinner she was the only talker, and after dinner she persuaded her son to go to bed, saying he needed plenty of sleep after such an awful day. He was only too glad to escape to his bedroom. 'Now we can talk, Lil,' she said, and they went off to the small study, where she hoisted herself on the table. Lil sat on the late husband's chair. The curtain wasn't drawn, and thus the moon shone on Margery's back.

'The last thing I expected,' said Margery.

'I expected it.'

'Why?' asked Margery, crossing her long legs.

'Because one is always afraid to lose the person who matters to one most.'

'I see what you mean, Lil. The last time I was over he told me he's leaving you five thousand pounds.'

'No consolation,' said Lil.

'You're a good looker. You won't be alone for long. Why don't you come over to Cannes? Plenty of room for you.'

'Never,' said Lil.

'You've become a sentimentalist. So he'll have a proper Catholic burial?' Lil nodded. 'Claud told me they went to confession and communion yesterday. How can that priest give him communion with you living with him?'

'He could,' said Lil quietly. 'The last two years there was nothing between us.'

'He became impotent?'

'He didn't,' said Lil, flushing. 'He always went to Mass, but never confessed or took communion. He used to tell Claud he was waiting for the appropriate moment, and none should hustle him. Two years ago he went to Father Turle, whose neck I could wring, and when he came back he said, "From now on we can stay together only as brother and sister".'

'Did he keep to it?'

'He kept to it.'

'And you didn't use your charms to make him snap out of it?'

'I respected him too much for that.'

'He was a strange man,' said Margery, getting off the table. 'Anything to drink?'

'I'll get some whisky,' said Lil.

Margery's eyes followed her to the door. Lil had become a soft fool. She shook her head, for Lil had already been a soft fool seventeen years ago when she fell desperately in love with her late husband, and gave up all her chances by turning herself into his slave, cook and maid of all work. There wasn't a man in the world for whom she, Margery, would have done that. Lil returned with a half empty bottle of whisky and two glasses on a tray.

'I want to talk to you about Claud,' said Lil.

'He'll be all right. House, farm and a nice sum of money. What else does he need?'

'Victor had one fear, namely his finding out.'

'Why should be find out, with Victor gone?'

'Walter is still around, and you know what an evil man he is.'

'We're all evil one way or the other,' said Margery complacently.

'Listen, Margery,' said Lil, standing up, now as tall as Margery seated on the table. 'Take Claud to Cannes straight after the funeral, keep him for a month or so. I'll hold the fort here, and if necessary I'll see Walter and frighten him.'

'How lucky I am that nobody can frighten me.'

Because you've no conscience, no heart, said Lil to herself. 'Margery, take him to Cannes. What's a month to you? Yet it can make all the difference. We owe it not so much to Victor's memory as to Claud. If the boy found out it would shatter him, a double blow he wouldn't recover from.'

'You're a sentimentalist, Lil. We recover from every possible blow. Think of all the blows I recovered from.'

'You're very resilient, Margery.'

'Thank God for that. You're awfully fond of Claud, aren't you?'

'I saw that boy growing up, he became part of my life. I don't want him to be hurt. Take him with you. No sacrifice for you, and while he's away I'll tidy everything up.'

'Frighten Walter and see he doesn't come near him. I'm not thinking of Victor. All right, I'll take him. No, best thing

25

if he comes out a day or two later. I want to prepare David for it.'

'He needs no preparation,' said Lil coldly.

'How little you know him,' said Margery, yawning. 'I'm going to bed, I'm done to the world. Flying always half kills me.' She started for the door, then turned back. 'If a man I cared for refused to sleep with me for whatever reason, I'd make life sheer hell for him till he changed his mind.'

'I repeat, I respected him too much.'

'That's the one thing I never did,' said Margery. 'Good night, Lil.'

Margery left the door open, and Lil listened to her footsteps as she climbed the stairs. Lil poured out a little whisky, drank it neat, then went out. This is over, she said half aloud. She looked into the library, the moonbeams were huge luminous shafts, she ought to draw the curtains, but she hadn't the strength left for it.

Wilf growled as she went past Claud's bedroom.

II

1

The hotel bedroom was long and narrow and smelt of Russian leather. The sun shone mercilessly on the bed. Its force woke David Woodlow who looked at his watch, only half past ten, so he closed his eyes determined to sleep till half past eleven, the usual time for him to get up. Already in his youth he had been told he had the head of an amiable bloodhound; now in his fifties it was even more pronounced. The chin sagged, and grey moustache and grey sideboards added to the effect. He didn't manage to fall asleep again, yet kept his eyes closed till he thought it was half past eleven. As a matter of fact it was only eleven twenty-five. He sighed because of the lost five minutes. He got out of bed, went to the window, and stared down on Cannes and the Mediterranean. You invariably expect to see Ulysses on the blue expanse, he said to himself, though you know he will never sail past. He moved to the table, took a cigarette from a packet, and lit up. Then he pushed the bathroom door open to run his bath. The hot water made a terrific racket as it filled the bath. With cigarette stuck to his lower lip he got into the hot water. When he finished the cigarette he aimed the stub at the lavatory. If it fell in his day would be pleasant; if he missed it, something annoying was in store for him. He aimed well which made him smile confidently.

When he was dressed (he wore a light grey suit) he left the room and, not bothering to take the lift, hurried downstairs. Mme Romei, the hotel-keeper, was seated at the reception desk, Modeste, her niece, sat at a smaller one, adding up bills. Modeste, as though her name had predestined her for it, was the poor relation and her aunt treated her thus. Mme Romei was in love with David, so English, so distinguished, and so intriguingly fascinating. Her dark eyes lit up, and she tried to smile engagingly as David said good morning to her. She was a short widow in her forties. The late M. Romei had died fifteen years ago. 'A widow must look after her interests,' she told the regular hotel guests whenever she raised the price. Had David made a pass at her, she would have repulsed him. But to dream of him as a perfect mate, that she was certain couldn't go against her interests.

'Did you sleep well, monsieur?'

'I always sleep well, the result of having a clear conscience.'

'If only every one of us could say that,' said Mme Romei, looking hard at Modeste who had shamed the family when she became an unmarried mother. The child was farmed out, and the aunt refused to let her marry the night porter, a student in the daytime, who was the child's father. In fact, she sacked him and he was only too glad to go. Poor Modeste had thought that her pregnancy would move her aunt, and force her to give in.

Nieces, thought Modeste sadly, after her stratagem had misfired, are no match for their aunts.

'It's such a beautiful day,' gushed Mme Romei.

'Indeed it is,' said David, and he gave Modeste a friendly glance as he passed her desk. You and I are kindred spirits in a sense, he wished to be able to say to her.

He took coffee and ate two croissants at the counter of a café near the hotel. Two tall, giggling Danish girls sat at the next table. The sun was even hotter, and there was no sea breeze, yet he strode fast to the house near the station, where Margery lived on the second floor. With all the huge modern buildings snow-white in the sun the yellow house looked old-fashioned, almost derelict. True on the ground floor was Alice's London Bar owned by Margery, but it opened only at four in the afternoon. Neither Margery nor David had the faintest idea who Alice had been. The Corsican who sold the bar to Margery couldn't enlighten them either. 'London' had been added by Margery. David mounted the steps spryly, not even stopping on the first floor landing to regain his breath.

Sylvie, Margery's *bonne*, let him in. Sylvie, he often said, must have been a prostitute in her attractive days. 'So what?' said Margery. 'She isn't now, and she cooks well.'

'Madame is in the drawing-room,' said Sylvie.

'How's your spine?'

'Hurts,' said Sylvie, who believed that her spine was rotting away.

'The doctor said there's nothing wrong with it.'

'What do doctors know?'

'All the X-rays agree there's nothing wrong with it, Sylvie.'

Sylvie gave him a sad and knowing smile, then opened the drawing-room door for him.

The drawing-room was atrociously furnished. Facing an imitation Louis XV sofa stood two large leather armchairs, between them a glass-topped table that had come from the bar downstairs. A rocking-chair was in one corner, a potted palm in the other, and under the chandelier was a round table with a chipped marble top. Margery reclined on the sofa, her long legs reaching to the armchair on the left. She wore white trousers and a lilac blouse. Her hair looked unbrushed. On the table a bottle of pastis, ice in a small bucket and a jug of water were beside a vast ashtray advertising a brand of whisky. Two hunting prints, also from the bar, where hung about a dozen or so, made the London appeal stronger. David sat down in the armchair farthest from her sandalled feet. 'Pastis?' she asked.

'Yes, please.'

'Help yourself to it,' she said, 'it's too hot to move.'

'Did the flight back tire you?'

'The stay too.'

'That was to be expected.'

She looked at him as he poured pastis into a glass. When he had dropped two lumps of ice into the glass she said, as venomously as she could, 'Your son is arriving tomorrow.' David poured water drop by drop into the glass. 'Didn't you hear me?' David drank a little before turning to her.

'You shouldn't use that word, Margery,' he said quietly.

'I wouldn't use it to anyone else, and certainly not to him.'

'If you use it once you can use it again,' he said, sitting

29

down. 'Why is Victor's son coming?'

'I'm your loyal friend, David,' said Margery. 'Lil thinks there's a danger of him finding out.'

'How can he?'

'Give me a little more pastis.' She watched him pouring it out. 'Lil fears Walter turning up. Victor is no longer there to kick him out.'

'Yes, Victor is somewhere else. I hope for his sake he isn't treated too brutally.'

Margery made an impatient gesture. 'Keep your wit to yourself. We didn't put his death into the papers. Lil's idea, but I think she was right. Still, people are bound to find out.'

'The whole idea was that people shouldn't find out.'

'Can't you understand that with Victor's death everything has changed? He can't protect the boy any more.'

'So the boy's coming here. I think I'll have a little more pastis.'

'Lil wants it, and it's only for a month. In the meantime she'll find out how the land lies, and will get rid of Victor's papers, correspondence, and if necessary beard Walter in his lair. She adores Claud.'

'I for one,' said David after a brief silence, 'don't really care. I paid so as not to have to care.'

'You only think of money.'

'And what about my career?'

'It was your wife's death that finished it.'

'Only in one sense. Anyway, we don't want to go over it again. I warn you, Margery, if that boy finds out the truth then I'm the only one who needn't blush.'

'I think you're the one who'd have to blush. You know why. It would break the boy's heart, Lil says.'

'I never knew that broken hearts mattered to you,' said David, laughing.

'Lunch is served,' said Sylvie, poking her head in.

The dining-room contained the furniture of the tenant whom Margery had succeeded, table, chairs and sideboard in dark oak from the rue du Faubourg-Saint-Antoine in Paris, giving the impression that even in two hundred years' time they would look as fresh from the shop as on the day they were bought. Invariably David looked at them in disgust before forgetting them.

Sylvie had remained attached to the cooking of the department of the Nord. The blistering sun of the South of France she ignored as she cooked. The meals she produced would have filled with joy a farmer's family snowed up in Flanders. Today it was carbonade, tomorrow would be pot-au-feu, and a pork stew the day after. She brought in the steaming dish with a triumphant smile which disappeared as she remembered her spine. Stooping, she left the room after she had served David and Margery.

'What matters to you and me,' Margery said, 'is that Claud should never know. That's why I agreed with Lil.'

'You'll put him up in the spare room?'

'Out of the question. I don't lead a mother's life.'

'You can be very amusing at times,' smiled David.

'I want him to stay in your hotel.'

'Never, Margery.'

'It won't make any difference to him since he suspects nothing. To you even less.'

'What about my father's heart?'

'You make me laugh. At the funeral some silly woman called Mrs Coke said to me, "Your husband will live on in your son. He resembles him strikingly".'

'That doesn't mean she's silly. If I showed the photograph of any stranger and said "That's my brother", people would immediately find a resemblance.'

'You book him a room for tomorrow in your hotel. You won't have to see more of him there than you would if he stayed here.'

'What will he think of Alice's London Bar?'

'He's too innocent to think anything. Besides, he's going to marry the Coke woman's daughter in the not-too-distant future. Once he's married we won't have to bother about him.'

'Because marriage solves everything, Margery?'

'Don't start going over it again. To me it's older than the Flood.'

'Ha, ha.'

Sylvie appeared with crème au caramel.

'I really can't,' said David.

'We can't hurt Sylvie's feelings,' said Margery.

'That's a good one,' laughed David, and ate the crème au caramel.

'I don't want to speed the departing guest,' said Margery after they had returned to the drawing room, 'but Michel is coming at three.'

'I'm off,' said David, and going down the stairs he said to himself, If only I could have felt like this about her when I met her twenty-four years ago.

He stopped in the doorway, wondering whether to go to the cinema or buy *The Times* and read it on the terrace of some café. He decided on buying the newspaper. Having bought it he went to a café beyond the station, a modest place where he could feel safe in that nobody he knew would pounce on him. There would be plenty later in the bar.

Sitting next to him on the terrace was a perspiring, fat woman dressed in a red dress with a boy of around nine, who looked bored stiff. David ordered a glass of beer, then settled down to read. Was he an exile, or an expatriate, or a refugee? All three, he smiled complacently. What sort of a lover was Michel? Margery said he was phenomenal, but she said that of any man while the affair lasted. He, too, must have been phenomenal before the Flood. He put down *The Times*, and there appeared before him a large café in the Place Pigalle, and he clearly saw three young officers seated at a table, one of whom was himself.

'Plenty of whores here,' said Walter Elking, looking round the café.

'We're in Pigalle,' said Victor Darnell.

David said nothing because of the immense amount of drink inside him.

They were in a gay mood, for their military career would soon be ending. They had seen a lot of fighting, from Normandy to the Rhine, and now they were in Paris for a few days pending their return to England. David smiled

vaguely, as if to hide his thoughts. He hadn't a high opinion
of Walter, and he wouldn't miss Victor once their roads
divided. It was easy for him, as he was the first to admit. His
father was a landowner in several counties, had sat in the
House of Commons as a Conservative MP, and his ambition
was that his only son should follow in his footsteps. David
was all for it, though with a vengeance in so far as he was
ambitious. For the father, the House had been a pastime and
a duty to himself and his position, whereas David wanted to
enter Parliament to make a spectacular political career.
Walter and Victor had similar backgrounds and their futures
looked pretty dim. Neither had any wealth behind him.
Walter seemed unaffected by it, but Victor hated his lack of
means. 'I wasn't born to fight for my daily bread,' he would
frequently observe. There were moments when he toyed with
the idea of staying on in the Army, but then the colonel
would say something he didn't like, which he considered as
proof of the Army being not for him. The three of them had
become close friends during their training in England, and
even closer during the campaign. David, who wasn't devoid
of shrewdness, was the first to guess that the great friendship
would cease on the day they were demobbed.

'How much do you think a whore costs for the night?'
Walter asked.

'Haven't the foggiest idea,' said David.

'I wouldn't pay a woman even if she were the only woman
in the world,' said Victor, patting his moustache. He was truly
handsome, Walter looked furtive, and David was already the
amiable bloodhound. At a nearby table sat four American
T-sergeants in whom the women were more interested than
they were in the three British officers.

'I bet she's English,' said Victor.

A strikingly tall girl had entered the café. She went
straight to the counter, where she shook hands with the two
barmen and also with a prostitute who sat on a barstool with
her back to the counter in order to study prospective customers
at leisure. David craned his neck to listen : the tall girl was
talking to the barmen in French without any trace of accent.

Suddenly she turned her head in David's direction. Their eyes met. He stood up and said, 'You're English, aren't you?'

'Not difficult to guess,' she said.

'Would you care to join us?' David asked.

'In a moment,' she said.

'She must be a whore too,' said Walter in a low voice.

'A lone woman in a Pigalle café at midnight couldn't be anything else,' said Victor, 'but I must admit she looks attractive in a way.'

'I'm the one who spoke to her,' said David.

'Which means,' laughed Walter, 'the first bash will be yours. Anyway, I'm not in the running.'

'I suppose a few packets of cigarettes will do the trick,' said David.

The tall girl detached herself from the bar, and came up to them. The three stood up. 'How do you do,' she said, signalling to a waiter who brought her a chair. She sat down and took a cigarette from Walter's packet. 'Players at last,' she said, and lit up. A cool customer, thought David. 'What are you drinking?' she asked.

'Brandy,' said David.

'I'll have brandy too.'

'I guessed at once you were English,' said Victor, 'but what are you doing here in Paris? Are you in the services?'

'Oh no. I was here during most of the war,' she said.

'Were you interned?' asked Walter.

'I managed not to be,' she said.

'How did you manage it?' asked Walter, leaning forward.

'Don't ask one question after the other,' said David, looking hard at Walter. You're not going to pinch her from me, his eyes said.

'I like answering questions,' she said. 'My name is Margery. Call me Margery.' She turned to Walter. 'I had a false French identity card, as simple as that.'

The next thing that fool of a Walter will ask, said David to himself, is what she's doing in a Pigalle café at night. 'How did the Germans treat you?' David asked, in order to stop Walter becoming tactless.

'We hadn't much to do with one another,' said Margery.

'You mean you were in hiding,' said Victor.

'It wasn't necessary,' said Margery. 'I can see you're all dying to know my story. I was the English governess in a French family in Amiens. I came over in '38 aged eighteen. When the Germans overran France I just couldn't get away or out. Luckily I found a protector who got me a French identity card. It was plain sailing after that. Not much of a story.' She gave them the smile that should stop them asking more questions. She didn't know Walter.

'Why are you in this café tonight?' he asked.

'This is really too much,' David exploded. 'I ask this lady to join us, and all you do is to put tactless stupid questions to her.' Walter blushed crimson, for he wasn't one who enjoyed a dressing down. David turned to Margery. 'Don't you know some other café round here, where we could drink in peace?'

'Dozens,' she said.

David called the waiter, paid for the drinks, and then, nodding to Victor, left the café with Margery. Only a few street lights were burning, the pavement and road were in a lamentable state, policemen were plentiful, and as David and Margery came out a jeep passed with American military police. At the corner were two English military policemen. Captain Woodlow pretended not to see them. In the café which Margery took him to, American sergeants predominated. Margery shook hands with waiters, barmen and women. David ordered brandy. Margery sat facing him, smoking and smiling.

'Are you always so hard on your friends?' she asked.

'Walter gets on my nerves. He's fundamentally vulgar and nasty.'

'What he wanted me to admit,' said Margery, 'was that I was no better than a common or garden prostitute.'

'But you're not,' said David stoutly.

'I live by it, but I'm not one really. With the war over I'm sure to find some job somewhere. If you're keen on me I'm quite willing to prostitute myself.'

35

David was embarrassed. She was a well-spoken girl, had a presence, in short, you didn't feel as a man should feel when in a prostitute's company. To court her, yes, to tell her to lie down and get on with the job, definitely no. 'I'd like that very much,' he murmured.

'Then let's go,' she said. 'Anyway, I'm half drunk.'

'Where do you live?'

'We're going to a hotel.'

In the street she walked beside him like any young woman being taken out. She took him to a sordid hotel in the rue Tholozé. The woman behind the desk received her with a huge smile, then said, 'You want number twelve, Mme Marge?'

'It's my favourite,' said Margery.

The old chambermaid who preceded them on the stairs called her Mme Marge too. Number twelve was a large room, with pink lamp shades, and narrow brass bed. 'We'll use the sofa, Annie,' said Margery to the chambermaid.

'I'll put a sheet on it,' said Annie, and went out to fetch it.

Margery stood with her back to the wide looking glass. David, still near the door, couldn't think of anything to say. Annie returned with a sheet. 'Tip her,' said Margery. He tipped her and Annie left. Margery locked the door. 'Undress,' she said, turning her back on him, and pulling her jumper over her head. Down came the skirt, underclothes followed, and she went to the sofa and lay down. 'I'm ready,' she said.

She was even thinner then he had expected. Her breasts were well developed, yet they couldn't destroy his first impression, namely that hers was the immature body of a very young girl who had grown too fast. David made love to her without the sense of liberation that makes one forget oneself. She was pretty passive, and her eyes declared that she had nothing to do with what went on. A bloody bad lay, he couldn't help thinking when he rose from the sofa. She went straight to the bidet, and talked to him while she washed herself.

'Were I a real one,' she said, 'I'd have asked for the money before, but I haven't the training for it.'

'How much would you like me to give you?' he asked, beginning to dress.

'Would a thousand francs be too much?' she asked, rising from the bidet. She used a clean towel, which Annie had brought, to wipe herself.

'Not at all,' he said, taking out his wallet. He put a thousand-franc note on the table. Was it little or much? He had no idea.

'Thank you,' she said, standing in front of him. 'You mustn't think that I'll go on with this sort of life. One has to watch one's step far too carefully. I'm not a registered whore, so I can't be seen in Pigalle too much or too often. The women here have their maquereaux, the police know them, so in their way they're protected. I'm not, and I don't want to be.'

'Can't the police burst into this hotel?'

'The patronne is well in with them. Have you a spare packet of Players?' He gave her one, then to his surprise she put her hand on his shoulder. 'I think I'm going to allow myself a little luxury. Stay here with me for the night if you can. All you have to do is to pay double for the room when you leave.'

David was moved, and so he stayed. The second time it was infinitely better. He didn't get much sleep because she talked nineteen to the dozen. 'I seldom have the opportunity to speak my own tongue,' she said. She was one of five sisters, their mother a naval officer's widow. Their brother had been sent to a good school, thus there was no money to educate the sisters. To become a governess abroad was deliverance for her.

'Were you here in Paris during most of the war?' David asked, saying to himself he was a bore like Walter.

'I told you I had a protector. I stayed with him in Amiens till the Liberation.'

'And then?'

'He was arrested as a collaborator. He's still in prison. I remained in the house, but his wife, who had run as far as the South of France when the Germans arrived, came back and

37

kicked me out. I came to Paris.'

'Will you go back to England?' The perfect Walter, he couldn't resist saying to himself.

'If some rich man marries me. As long as I have to look after myself I prefer to stay here.' She laughed. 'My formative years were spent in France.'

At seven o'clock he got up to go. In the morning light she looked defenceless and young. When he was dressed he went to the bed, and kissed her on the forehead. 'Will you be around tonight?' he asked.

'Towards midnight in the café where we met. Don't forget to pay for the room. If you see Annie tip her again.'

The Boulevard de Clichy and Pigalle were a sordid and sobering sight. I spent the night with a whore, David said to himself while searching for a taxi. Admittedly a nice one, yet a whore all the same. A fat prostitute accosted him. 'No merci, madame,' he said, then nearly laughed. What right had he to say no merci so indignantly, when coming straight from another?

That night he didn't go back to Pigalle. In the afternoon he looked up a schoolmate of his who was at the Embassy, and who insisted on their dining together in a black market restaurant. From the restaurant David went straight to bed.

A few months later in London he asked Walter to lunch at his club. They had been demobbed, their roads had parted, hence he saw no reason for not spending a couple of hours in Walter's company: probably their last meeting for a long time. Walter had got a job in a stockbroker's office. When they reached their second brandy Walter said, 'You remember Margery, the tall girl we met in Pigalle?'

'I do,' said David. 'Why?'

'Victor and I went back to that café the night after. She came in, sat with us, then I laid her in some awful hotel.' To his astonishment David felt a pang of jealousy. Though his mind said that you can't feel jealous of a prostitute, the sensation refused to leave him. 'She asked for two thousand francs,' Walter continued, 'but I gave her only a thousand.'

'Half past two. Sorry, Walter, I have an appointment at three.'

The fat woman and the boy left the café terrace. David folded *The Times*, paid for his beer, but left *The Times* behind on the table. You can, he thought as he walked away, conjure up the past, yet you can't put life into it. The Margery of Pigalle was unconnected with the Margery he would shortly see in Alice's London Bar.

The heat hadn't let up, and he wiped his forehead several times before he reached the bar. The bar was rigged up like a London pub between the wars, but the London pub was only the foundation. Once you took in the pub counter and the hunting prints, not to mention the white dog and the black dog and the white horse, you realised you were far from England. The curtains and the lampshades, the red carpet, too, were for a clientele that didn't stick to licensing hours. At the counter was a hefty man drinking stout. Alfred, the barman, was gazing into space, which meant that the hefty man had been boring him for a considerable time. The hefty man turned to David as he reached the bar.

'Twenty-four hours ago,' he said, 'I was drinking the same stout in my local in Bolton. As I was saying to George here,' he pointed at Alfred, 'what's the good of travelling.'

'I ask myself the same questions,' said David. 'Alfred, is madame still upstairs?'

'I haven't seen her go out,' said Alfred. 'Mme Formby is over there.'

David nodded, then went to Elfrida Formby's table. Not that he enjoyed being with her, but it was preferable to an inane chat with the hefty man. She sat behind the *Herald-Tribune*, and looked up only when he had addressed her. Elfrida was Margery's sole bosom friend, their totally different past and present notwithstanding. Elfrida had been married to a man forty years older than herself; when he had died she came to the South of France in the hope of finding plenty of fun at last. However, she hadn't the gift for fun, and soon she lapsed into a routine she would have abhorred even while the forty-years-older husband lasted. She envied and venerated Margery because she seemed to have her finger on the pulse of life. She lived through her, and if Margery changed her lover the fifteen-years-younger Elfrida was as excited as if she herself had chosen a new one.

'I wasn't lucky last night,' sighed Elfrida, who took the bus once a week to the Casino Municipal of Nice, where she risked small sums at roulette. She was back at midnight to watch the late night fun at Alice's London Bar, fun into which she didn't manage to enter.

'If one's a resident one shouldn't gamble,' said David. 'What will you have?'

'I've had tea, I don't feel like a drink yet.'

'Alfred,' called David, 'bring me a marc.'

'Yes, Monsieur David.'

'I'm sure,' said David to Elfrida, 'I'll start believing I'm David of Angers.'

As Elfrida had no idea who David of Angers was she gave him a vague smile that she considered attractive. Elfrida had a flushed complexion and violet-coloured eyes.

'Margery tells me her son is coming over for a month,' she said. 'So thrilling.'

'There's nothing thrilling about a grown-up son.'

'How can you say that? Anyway, you haven't any children.'

'An outsider can judge much better,' said David.

'You've got an answer to everything.' She leaned across the table, and David thought there was too much powder on her chin. 'Her husband was a great friend of yours, Margery tells me. You were in the war together.'

'Haven't seen him for donkey's years.'

'How's that?'

'Wartime friendships are like wartime marriages, my dear.'

'You're incorrigible,' giggled Elfrida, who was proud of her sense of humour. 'Here's Margery.'

Now wearing lilac trousers and a white shirt, Margery went

up to the bar, Michel in her wake. He was a lawyer from Nice, dark haired with a fine Roman nose. Margery liked his bushy eyebrows. The hefty man turned to Michel.

'Twenty-four hours ago,' he said, 'I was drinking the same stout in my local in Bolton. What's the good of travelling, eh?'

'I do not speek anglais, monsieur,' said Michel, bowing. Then he waved to David. 'Marge,' he said in French, 'I think I must leave you. Tomorrow?' His eyes declared that he wanted tomorrow to roll on as quickly as possible.

'Alas, not tomorrow, mon chéri,' said Margery. 'My son is arriving. Oh, why can't you come at night?'

'I can't leave my pregnant wife alone.'

'The day after tomorrow it will be all right again,' said Margery. She gazed at him fondly, for the love of a man who was nearly twenty years younger moved her irresistibly.

Michel left, and Margery called to David, 'Have you fixed it with your hotel?'

'Haven't had time.'

'You've more time than anybody I know, David.'

'I'm going,' said David, 'straight to the hotel to fix it.'

'Will you be back tonight?'

'I've nowhere else to go,' David laughed.

'He's such fun,' said Elfrida, watching him go to the door. Two handsome young men held the door open for him.

'You're not going,' the taller of them said.

'I'm gone,' said David.

'Mon petit chéri, isn't he absolutely sweet,' said the other young man.

The hotel was cool. Though a daughter of the South, Mme Romei disliked the sun. The shutters in the hall were still closed, and Modeste sat behind the big desk, which meant that her aunt was having her siesta. Modeste stood up, and David thought for perhaps the hundredth time that, if she weren't under her aunt's thumb, she could turn into a pretty girl. Her raven black hair and cloudy grey eyes he found remarkable, and when she smiled, which she did only away from her aunt, any professional beauty might have envied her teeth. She was just over twenty, he had known her for ten years, and had been a silent and distant witness of her fall. He was sure that the night porter student had been relieved when Mme Romei refused to let him marry her niece. On no account would he have told that to Modeste.

'Have you a room vacant tomorrow?' he asked. 'The son of a friend of mine is coming to Cannes for a month. A very young man, so any room will do, but don't put him on my floor. I don't want him to be in and out of my room.'

'We've a small room on the fourth floor. It overlooks the courtyard.'

'Rather dark. Still, young people are not that fussy.'

'My room is pretty dark.' Modeste smiled. 'She's coming.' The smile went.

Mme Romei stepped out of the lift, Modeste moved to the smaller desk, and David went out into the evening that was slowly gathering beneath rosy clouds.

It was a rule of his not to get too drunk before it was time to fall into bed. So he walked for an hour, stopping in front of shop windows to look at goods he would never buy. He liked a jeweller's dazzling display on the Croisette because he couldn't think of anyone to whom he would care to offer a bracelet or a necklace. He strolled on. The light clouds were losing their colour, and the sea was streaked with purple. He found himself in front of the Carlton Hotel. He kept away from the Carlton Bar and the Casino, believing that if he went into them he would run into people who had belonged to his brief great period. I am a fool, he said to himself. Those people are either dead or have forgotten me, and if they aren't dead and they still remember me they won't come rushing to Cannes in order to bring back the past. As he entered the bar he thought of an old painter he knew in London who went regularly to the Café Royal in the hope of seeing old cronies whose obituary notices he had read and forgotten long ago.

'A large whisky, please,' said David to the barman.

Two young women stood at the bar, and he was almost certain they were the two Danes he had seen in the café where he had taken his breakfast. A man detached himself from the other end of the counter. 'David,' he said. 'Fancy running into you after all these years.'

'Hullo, Hector,' David said, cursing himself for being there.

'What are you doing here? Live here?'

'Part of the year. What will you have?'

'Barman, bring me over my drink, please,' said Hector, a stout man with a bulbous nose. He and David had sat in the House of Commons at the same period. 'I'm so pleased to see you, David. What about dining together? My wife will be down in a moment.'

'I'm awfully sorry, but I have a dinner engagement.'

'Can't you put it off?'

'Honestly I can't.'

'I often think of our great days, but how short they were.'

'I had three years of it, that's all.'

'And you never stood again.'

'I never stood again. One defeat was enough.'

'In politics defeats don't count.'

'In private life they do. You're in business now, if I remember rightly.'

'When I was beaten I decided to chuck it. All I ever got out of it was being PPS for a short spell. Now I'm a director of three companies. What are you doing, old David?'

'Beautifully nothing,' said David, and saw that Hector didn't care for that. 'Indeed it was nice to see you. Alas, I must be off.' Hector said that his wife would be down in a moment. 'So sorry, I'm late already.'

'Ring me when you're in town.'

David nodded, hurried out, and never stopped till he reached the rue d'Antibes, where he went into a small bistrot and had a large whisky. The other customers consisted of two masons. No more bars on the Croisette for me, said David to himself. Then he shrugged his shoulders, thinking that running into Hector and his like didn't even ruffle the surface any more. No anxiety is left if you know where you stand. And where did he stand? Nowhere, he said half aloud, smiling broadly, and the nearer mason beamed on him.

He dined in a small restaurant not far from Alice's London

43

Bar, the food being a mixture of Provençal and Italian cooking. A fat, retired French couple dined at the next table. They came every night, David every second night or so. By now he and they were on nodding terms without ever exchanging a word.

'I'm waiting for September to go to Tours to stay with our daughter,' said the wife. 'I won't have to eat noodles every night there.'

'When you come back in October you'll have noodles every night again,' said the husband.

Nice people, David said to himself as he left.

Alice's London Bar was crowded. Margery was behind the bar with Alfred the barman. That woman will never lose her personality, David thought as he pushed his way to the bar. 'Is the room booked?' she asked. David nodded. The customers were a mixed lot, in that a definite dividing line existed between those who sat at tables and those who clustered round the bar. The seated customers were mostly English and Americans, a lot of beachcombers really, David thought them. Artists who wouldn't go far, people who were distantly connected with the film world and were usually out of jobs, a retired jockey with his much younger wife whom David remembered as a bar customer before the jockey found and married her, a Mrs Vickers who was generally drunk and silent, also Mr Gillies, who had spent half his life in different jails, accompanied by his German wife, a lesbian who picked up girls at the bar under the friendly gaze of her husband. At the bar stood women ready to go with any man or woman for money, a small group of male homosexuals with whom Margery enjoyed flirting, and riff raff whom you hardly had to fear or take seriously. Margery welcomed anybody as long as there was no fear of drug peddling. In every sense she was on the right side of the law.

David sat down at a table near the bar. Alfred brought him a whisky bottle and a syphon. 'See that little fellow standing near the red-haired girl?' Alfred whispered. 'He's an English gangster.'

'How do you know that?'

44

'He told me.'

'I wouldn't trust him. Looks a perfect liar.'

Alfred returned to the bar unconvinced.

Elfrida made her entrance, her countenance showing she had not forgotten her losses at roulette. She sat down beside David. Alfred brought a glass, and David asked, 'How did you lose last night?' because he couldn't think of anything to say to her.

'I was playing the voisins of zero. No luck. You know, David,' she put her hand on his sleeve, 'I can't understand why you come here every night.'

'What are you doing here every night?'

'Because I enjoy the motley crowd.'

'I come because I don't enjoy it.'

'You are a one,' she laughed. 'Look at that girl over there. I know you'd call her a tart, yet she gets more fun out of life than either of us.'

'That girl, if you want to know, tried to kill herself about a year ago because her great love . . .'

'Left her?'

'Was locked up for ten years for taking part in a hold-up. Now she's looking for a new great love. She believes that this is the right place to find him.'

'Nevertheless,' said Elfrida firmly, 'her life isn't unexciting.'

David looked at her flushed face, remembering Margery's saying many months ago that Elfrida was after him. 'Not on your life,' David had answered.

A girl appeared, her hair streaming down to her waist. Mrs Gillies half rose to have a better look at her. The girl spoke to Margery, who wrote something on a slip of paper. The girl took it and left. David frowned, for hadn't he told Margery a thousand times to stop acting as a go-between. She can't shake off the habit, he muttered under his breath.

'David, you look so farouche,' said Elfrida.

'Have a drink.'

'I don't want to get tiddly.'

'Why?'

'You do ask funny questions,' said Elfrida.

Marcel, the second barman, made his appearance. This meant that Margery could leave. Marcel went behind the bar, and David idly watched as he and Margery went through the lists of drinks served and not yet paid for. When they had finished Margery beckoned to Elfrida and David, and both of them followed her out of the bar. Upstairs in her drawing-room the three chatted and drank till three in the morning.

'I'm going, too, David,' said Elfrida.

She said that every night, and every night David parted from her in the doorway. A taxi was waiting for her. 'Can I give you a lift?' she called. He strode on, pretending not to hear her.

Funny, he thought, approaching his hotel, that I should never remember what Margery, Elfrida and I talk about. There must be some occult reason for it, or perhaps no reason whatever. The night porter let him in, an old man with sad eyes and a drooping white moustache. Mme Romei was taking no more risks.

My domain, said David half aloud as he entered his bed-room. He drank a little whisky, then got into bed, and read till he felt sleep enveloping him. He dropped the book, and closed his eyes in the hope of not waking before half past eleven.

3

'If I must go I'll travel in the Mistral,' Claud declared to Lil. 'The name is too fascinating.'

Three days later he sat in the Mistral speeding to Cannes. Lil had driven him to Dover with Wilf in the back of the car, and in Dover the dog never looked up while Claud patted him.

'He knows,' said Lil.

She kissed Claud on the forehead, put Wilf on the lead, and pulling him hard she went back to the car.

Claud glanced round the carriage and then at the window

beyond which the landscape was rushing backwards, too fast
for anything to be seen. Opposite him sat an old man,
blowing cigar smoke. In another seat slept a tall girl who had
begun sleeping when the train pulled out of the Gare de Lyon.
Claud sat back, and thought of his dead father. The sole
reason he had agreed to go to his mother was because of the
silly notion that while he was abroad Mr Darnell would
change his mind, come out of the tomb, and be there on his
return to start their old life all over again. He knew it couldn't
be, yet he saw no reason why he shouldn't dream of it.

Ludmilla hadn't been pleased. 'Mother says it's such a
vulgar place nowadays,' she said. When Mrs Coke came in
through the french window, wearing her gardening gloves, she
was askance to hear he was going to such a town. 'And so
soon after your father's death.'

'Were he alive I shouldn't go,' said Claud.

'Of course, your mother is there,' said Mrs Coke, 'but she
should have stayed here with you.'

Claud said his mother couldn't stay. They asked him why
she couldn't, and the only answer he could think of was that
she had said so. Ludmilla saw him to the gate, got into the
car, they necked, but when he touched her breast she said,
'Don't spoil it, Claud.'

The girl in the corner woke up, looked first at the old man,
then at Claud, let out a deep sigh, and fell asleep again. Claud
followed suit in a little while. He opened his eyes only after
Marseilles : old man and girl were gone. 'How blue it is,' he
said as the train seemed to fly past the sea.

At Cannes station he immediately spotted his mother,
towering above the little crowd. He went up to her, and
craning his neck he kissed her on the cheek. 'Had a good
journey?' Margery asked, then without waiting for an answer,
'Is this all the luggage you have?'

'It's plenty for me.'

'You know what you need, Claud. I'm taking you to the
hotel where you'll be staying...'

'Aren't I staying with you, mother?'

'Not enough room in my flat. You'll leave your suitcase,

47

then we'll go to the flat, and you'll dine with me. I've got a lot to tell you.'

Neither spoke in the taxi, and when they reached the hotel she exclaimed, 'I completely forgot. You stay here. I shan't be long.'

Thus Claud was left alone with Modeste who sat behind the large desk, since Mme Romei was having her siesta. Claud smiled at her, she smiled back, then bent over the ledger. I ought to speak to her, thought Claud.

'Mademoiselle.' Modeste looked up. 'On which floor is my room?' he asked in halting French.

'On the fourth, monsieur. Do you want to go up?'

'Not now, as I'm waiting for my mother to come back.'

'I understand, monsieur.'

They lapsed into silence, however continued to smile at one another. This time it was Modeste who thought she ought to speak to him. 'Monsieur David is out,' she observed.

'Who is he?'

'He has a very difficult family name which I can't pronounce I'll write it down for you.'

She wrote Woodlow on a slip of paper. Claud read it, then said, 'I don't know him.'

Modeste blushed, believing she had made some gaffe. Hadn't her aunt told her when she started to work for her that one should never speak to one client about another? She tried to excuse herself. M. David had booked the room, so she was entitled to think that the young man knew him. 'I thought you knew him, monsieur. We French always believe that all the English know each other. Stupid, isn't it? I'd laugh if I went abroad and were told that all the French knew each other.'

'Have you been to England?'

She didn't have time to say she hadn't, because Margery re-appeared and whisked Claud off. The taxi dropped them in front of the old yellow house.

'Alice's London Bar,' Claud read, getting out of the cab.

'Tell you about it upstairs,' said Margery.

'M. David telephoned to say he couldn't come tonight as

he had to go to Nice,' said Sylvie, opening the door for them.

'Who's M. David, mother?' Claud asked. 'The girl in the hotel mentioned him, thought I knew him.'

'He's a friend of mine, and he booked the room for you.'

So he funked it, said Margery to herself. Elfrida will be disappointed. She had asked them both to dinner since she didn't look forward to dining à deux with Claud. 'Have a drink, Claud. Never tried pastis?'

Claud liked pastis, and Margery waited till he had his second.

'That bar downstairs is mine,' she said.

'Oh, is it?'

'I run it myself.'

'Why haven't you told me before?'

'Victor didn't want me to.'

'Father said you lived here because of your health.'

'Call the bar my occupational therapy,' Margery laughed. 'I don't want you to go there at night, Claud. Go in the daytime, but, I repeat, not at night. One can't choose the clientele, and the people who go to bars at night aren't the sort I want you to know.'

'Anyway, I'm accustomed to go to bed at ten, a real country bumpkin.'

'Do you really want to carry on the farm?' He nodded firmly. 'Lil says you shouldn't because you're not really made for that kind of life.'

'It was father's wish,' said Claud. Margery, hearing the door bell ring, sighed her relief.

Elfrida wore a white dress in which she saw herself as a young, attractive thing. 'So this is your son, Margery,' she gushed. 'Looks like you.'

'Everybody tells me I look like my father,' said Claud.

'As I don't know your father I can't judge,' said Elfrida. 'Sorry, I forgot.'

'Forgot what?' asked Margery, who was thinking of Michel.

'That your husband died the other day,' said Elfrida.

'We don't need to be reminded of it,' said Margery, thinking of David.

Elfrida sat down. Margery remained standing, Claud too, and Elfrida searched for words, any words, to break the sudden silence. At such moments she hated her great friend because she had the knack of embarrassing you. 'Are you,' Elfrida asked, 'at a university?'

'I'm not,' said Claud. 'My father wanted me to be a farmer, so I'll be a farmer. A farmer doesn't need to go to a university.'

'I thought that all young people went to a university,' said Elfrida.

'I must be the exception,' said Claud.

Elfrida felt at her ease, for she had done her duty. 'When's David coming, Marge?'

'He's not coming,' said Margery. 'He rang up while I was out to say he couldn't.'

David again, thought Claud.

'I'm so disappointed,' said Elfrida.

'You'll see him downstairs,' said Margery.

'Dinner is served,' announced Sylvie. She let out a cry of pain as she threw the door wide open.

'What's wrong with her?' Claud asked.

'Nothing,' said Margery.

There was little talk at dinner, though Elfrida did her best. The surroundings were too new and strange for Claud to think of anything to say, and Margery was too deep in her thoughts to be aware of her son's presence. She was of Elfrida's, but that didn't count. Suddenly she looked up from her plate. 'What did you say, Elfrida?'

'I was saying to your son that in July and August the Coast is insufferable.'

'It won't worry Claud,' said Margery. 'He won't be here by then.'

'I'm staying just for a month,' said Claud as if to reassure his mother.

'I honestly can't understand how David can stick it in summer,' said Elfrida.

'He's impervious to his surroundings,' said Margery.

'I'm not,' said Elfrida.

'We know that, darling,' smiled Margery. 'That's why you

live here as though you were still living in Esher.'

'You lived in Esher?' asked Claud.

'While my husband was alive,' said Elfrida. 'You know Esher?'

'Lil was born there.'

'Who's Lil?' Elfrida asked.

'His housekeeper,' said Margery.

'Much more than that,' said Claud.

'She's a grand person,' said Margery, glancing at her watch. 'You two have coffee, I must go downstairs.'

'Can't I have just a look at your bar?' asked Claud. 'I'm dying to see it.'

'Five minutes, that's all,' said Margery. 'Have coffee, then bring him down, Elfrida.'

Left alone Elfrida and Claud had nothing more to say. However, silence invariably unnerved Elfrida, so she found herself asking Claud to tea on the next day. Claud accepted, and she explained how to get to the gigantic block of flats in which she lived. This took ten long minutes. At the end of them she sighed her relief because they could go down to the bar without her having given away how difficult it was to talk to an unknown young man. 'This is the bar,' she said superfluously as they went in. 'David is over there. Let's go straight to him.'

'But mother is behind the bar,' said Claud.

'She doesn't like to be disturbed when she works,' said Elfrida, gazing at David. He stood up. 'This is Claud Darnell, Margery's son.'

'How do you do,' said David, and shook his hand. 'Sit down both of you.'

'Mother told me not to stay more than five minutes.'

'Why?' said David. 'She wants to change your nappies?' Claud laughed. 'Whisky?'

'A little please,' said Claud, who thought he liked David a lot.

'You should have dined with us,' said Elfrida reproachfully.

'I couldn't make it,' said David. 'Had a good journey, young man?'

'A very fast one. I came in the Mistral.'

'I'm told it's always full of Marseillais pickpockets,' said David.

'They left me alone,' said Claud, warming to David. 'I'm staying in the same hotel as you, sir.'

'It's a good hotel,' said David.

'I've asked Claud to tea tomorrow, David. Come too.'

'I don't take tea,' said David.

'You can have whisky.'

'Too early for whisky.'

'So you won't come.'

'I'm afraid not.'

'Look at that,' Claud exclaimed.

A man and a woman were having a fight at the bar. Alfred heaved himself over the counter to separate them, and did it with praiseworthy skill and rapidity, so that within a few seconds both were evicted. 'If they must fight,' said Alfred, 'they should do it in their home if they've got one.'

'Happens very seldom here,' said loyal Elfrida to Claud.

'That's the woman you envied last night for her exciting life, Elfrida,' laughed David.

A truly amusing man, thought Claud.

'Claud, your five minutes are up,' said Margery coming to the table.

'Can't I have another five minutes?'

'I prefer you to go. Come to lunch at half past one, but you'll have to leave before three.'

'Don't forget you're coming to tea tomorrow,' said Elfrida.

'How do I get to the hotel from here, sir?' Claud asked.

David explained, Claud left, and was astonished by the heat still lingering in the street, also by the stars that seemed more numerous than in England. He pushed the hotel door open, expecting to see Modeste. The night porter sat behind the desk, reading a newspaper. A bit of an anticlimax, thought Claud. He had forgotten his room number, the porter looked unhurriedly through the ledger, and before he could find his name Modeste came in from the street. She wore a light blue dress with red collar and cuffs. She was made up, looking different from the young woman he had seen behind the desk.

'This monsieur can't remember his room number,' said the night porter.

'I'll show him to his room,' said Modeste, leaning over the desk and taking the key.

The lift was narrow, and thus they were close to each other, which Claud found agreeable. Why couldn't she ask him to tea instead of that flush-faced friend of his mother? 'I met M. David,' he said.

'Oh, you have?' said Modeste. 'We're all very fond of him. He's been here ever since I can remember.' They got out of the lift. 'There's your room, monsieur. I hope the lift won't disturb you. Good night.'

Claud wished her good night. Before putting the key into the lock he looked back, and their eyes met because she had done the same. He entered his room mighty pleased with himself; but what did she mean about the lift disturbing him? He was soon to find out. His window overlooked the narrow courtyard, and the lift shaft was, as it were, stuck to the wall opposite and when the lift moved it whined like a child. Nonetheless, the lift didn't disturb him : he fell asleep the moment he got into bed. He dreamed he was walking in the garden with Mr Darnell. 'How could you do that to me, father?' Claud asked. Mr Darnell smiled mysteriously and said not a word.

In Alice's London Bar Margery said to David, 'Did you like him?'

'A nice young man.'

'Blood is thicker than water.'

'That's a good one,' laughed David.

III

When he got back to the hotel that night David forgot to have his nightcap. He sat on the bed, one shoe off, the other still on, and his thoughts far back in time.

His father died two years after David was demobbed, and he inherited the estates. The first thing he did was to take a flat in London not too far from the Mother of Parliaments, so as to be nearby when the call came. One morning he was rung up by Victor Darnell, whom he hadn't seen for a while. 'Come and have breakfast,' he said into the mouthpiece. Victor turned up shortly afterwards.

'How are things?' David asked.

'Rotten.'

'No job?'

'The jobs I'm offered are humdrum and boring.'

'So you do nothing?'

'I was born to do nothing.'

In those days David couldn't understand yet that doing nothing was an occupation of sorts.

They finished breakfast, and David said he was driving down to the house he owned near Dover, and a farm too. He hadn't been there since before the war. 'Why don't you come with me, Victor? We'll be back in the evening.'

'I'd like to,' said Victor.

It was a warm autumn day, and during the journey Victor expounded his theories about himself and life. David listened fascinated, for whatever you thought of it Victor's mind worked in an original fashion. His grandfather had made a fortune which his father spent, consequently there was nothing left for Victor to do.

'I don't follow you,' said David.

'But it's simple enough. There was no fortune when my grandfather was born. Got that?' David nodded. 'Had he had my father's temperament he couldn't have done anything because there was nothing to spend yet. Because he hadn't my father's temperament he made the fortune. That's clear, isn't it?' David nodded again. 'Thus he gave my father the opportunity to spend it. As I've the temperament of neither of them there is nothing left for me to do.'

'You could try to make a fortune,' said David.

'You don't listen, David. I can't make a fortune because I'm not like my grandfather, and I'm not like my father either.'

'If your father had made the fortune would you spend it?'

'What I'm trying to explain is that I wouldn't. It's not in me the same way as making a fortune isn't in me either. Got it at last?'

'I think so, and you think that absolves you from doing anything in life.'

'Precisely.'

'How are you going to live? . . . Look at that bloody woman, the way she overtook me.'

'I don't know how I'm going to live. That's why I'm so depressed. I wish I'd the knack to embezzle or cheat or rob or steal, but I haven't.'

'In your place, Victor, I'd become a civil servant and kill time till my pension is due.'

'I don't know how to kill time.'

'Don't say that so aggressively,' laughed David. 'Past opening time, we'll stop at that pub.'

The barmaid was remarkably tall. While serving them she smiled at David, her smile unconnected with whatever thoughts or ideas she harboured.

'Remember Margery from Pigalle, Victor?'

'Vaguely. Walter and I went back the next day, and Walter went with her.'

'Walter told me.'

'When they came back she asked if I wanted to go with her. I said I never paid a woman.'

55

'What did she say?' asked David, looking at the barmaid. Their eyes met and she gave him the same smile.

'She said she understood me. Then Walter went away and we remained chatting for quite a while. She said something I haven't forgotten. If there had been no war she would never have discovered that she could prostitute herself. If there hadn't been my father and grandfather I'd be working hard in some office this very minute.'

'She didn't look like a prostitute,' said David, 'but do you know why we think that? In our snobbish fashion we were impressed by her carriage, manners and voice.'

'I'm not so certain,' said Victor. 'I was impressed by her as a person.'

'Time we moved on.'

As a final test David looked at the barmaid again, and received the same smile.

They reached the house towards noon. David's eyes surveyed the farm buildings, the trees and garden with little pleasure. 'Never liked the place,' he said. They walked to the farmer's house, out came the farmer's wife who had no idea who David was, and thought that Victor was the more important of the two. When David introduced himself she went to fetch the key of the 'big house', as she called it. Accompanying them across she urged David to find a tenant for it because left on its own the house would crumble

'I'll think about it,' said David.

Victor found the big house enchanting. David opened doors without bothering to see what lay behind them, whereas Victor rushed up and down the stairs, looking into every nook and corner, his eyes shining, and he seemed happier than David had ever seen him. The farmer's wife asked whether David would like to see her husband. David said some other time, and she left them, asking them to leave the key in the lock so that she could collect it later on. 'Don't forget, Mr Woodlow, that this house will fall down if nothing is done about it.'

'I won't forget,' said David. He waited for her to be gone. 'I'll sell it, the farm too. Don't like this place at all.'

'How can you say that? It's a wonderful place.'

'Nothing wonderful about it. I'm a Norfolk man, and this means nothing to me.'

'Why don't you give it to me, David, if it means nothing to you.'

David thought Victor was joking, but as he looked at him he saw Victor was in deadly earnest. 'One doesn't give houses away, Victor.'

'You said you didn't want it. You don't need the money you'd get for it, so why can't you give it to me? I'd live here and be the happiest man in the world. I'd even earn a living to keep this house going. When the farmer's lease expires I'll run the farm, and . . . give it to me, David.'

David was disgusted. You can ask a friend for a loan since money is impersonal; you can't ask a friend for an object, as it may have a sentimental value; to ask him for a house, even if he doesn't care for it, is just not done. 'Why don't you ask a shipowner for the present of a ship, Victor?'

'I don't know any shipowners,' said Victor.

'Lucky shipowners,' laughed David.

'What difference would giving me this house make to your life?'

'None, but one doesn't give houses away. Anyhow, I know you're joking. We'll drive into Dover and have lunch.'

David started for the door, and waited outside for Victor, who remained behind. 'Hurry,' David called, 'I want to lock up.' Victor came at last, reminding David of a dog expecting punishment.

'It's no good,' said Victor when they drove off.

'What do you mean by no good?'

'Breaking down the wall behind which men of property hide.'

'You're incorrigible,' said David, deciding that from now on he would see as little of Victor as possible.

The lunch in Dover was not a success, as Victor sulked, his expression that of one to whom some awful injustice has been done. During the drive back he shrouded himself in gloomy silence. David felt deep relief when Victor left him in London, without a word of thanks for the outing. What a depressing outing, thought David. In order to cheer himself up, next day he took the Golden Arrow to Paris.

He could scarcely recognise the town. All marks of the occupation had disappeared, the streets were well paved, the City of Light sparkled, and after the home restrictions he gorged himself in restaurants. On the second evening of his stay he passed a bar near the Madeleine and, feeling like a drink, he pushed the door open. The bar was in semi-darkness, the curtains were of heavy crimson velvet, the discreet lamps lit the place up just enough to give an impression of secret and stolen love. Two women who appeared to be symbols of it were on this side of the bar, apparently waiting to be picked up; on the other side towered Margery.

'Hullo,' she said, 'I recognised you at once.'

'I'm glad to see you again,' said David, and the two women turned to smile at him. 'What are you doing here?'

'I'm a sort of manageress. It's a very good job. Have a drink, you're my guest. I mean for the first one.'

While she got the drinks a prosperous looking man with an imposing belly came in, and one of the women sat down with him at a table near the curtains. David gazed at Margery, surprised by the pleasure he felt in seeing her.

'How did you find this place?' she asked.

A waiter bobbed up from behind a crimson curtain at the other end of the bar to serve the man and the woman with him. 'Jacques,' called the woman who had remained at the counter, 'can I have a pernod too?'

'You can,' said the man with the imposing belly.

'I came past,' said David, 'and came in because I wanted a drink. Fate.'

'I've been here nearly two years,' said Margery. 'I'm happy here. The days when you knew me are over. Are you alone?' David said he was. 'I can recommend the girl next to you. She's very nice and won't fleece you. A couple of drinks and then you can make your own arrangement.'

'I want to make my own arrangement with you.'

'How nicely you said that, but, my dear, I can't leave before midnight, and by then I'll be dog-tired.'

'Never mind, I'll come back before midnight.'

'You're a dear,' she said. 'I must warn you you might be wasting your time.'

'Why? Have you somebody else?'

'I'm free. That's the fun of working here.'

A new young woman put in an appearance, followed by an earnest-looking man with a grey waistcoat. They sat down, and the woman at the counter joined them. 'That chap,' said Margery, 'must always have two.'

David went to dine, and was back well before midnight. The bar was crowded, yet at first glance he saw that all the customers there had a similar purpose. The women looked ready, the men eager. Beside Margery stood an ample woman, wearing jewels and watching the customers with an eagle eye. 'Mireille,' said the woman to a girl in a black dress, 'your friend telephoned to say he'll be here at one. Be patient.'

'Mme Hermine,' said Margery to the woman, 'this monsieur is a friend from England.'

'Vous êtes le bienvenu, monsieur,' Mme Hermine said ceremoniously.

Margery's eyes signalled to David who asked Mme Hermine to have a drink. Margery's eyes expressed her gratitude.

'Do you think I can leave?' she asked.

'By all means,' said Mme Hermine. 'I hope we'll see you again, monsieur.'

'I like it very much here,' said David.

'Yvonne,' said Mme Hermine to a large-bosomed short woman, 'if you're interested in a partouse ring this number.'

'Not tonight,' said Yvonne. 'I'm waiting for someone.'

'I'll have to find somebody else,' sighed Mme Hermine.

'It's a sort of a brothel, isn't it?' said David as he and Margery came out of the bar.

'You mustn't say that,' laughed Margery. 'All brothels are closed in France and Navarre. Call it a bar where it's easy to find what you need. Mme Hermine used to keep a brothel in Nantes, so she has the necessary experience to run such a bar. I'm learning a lot from her. Where are we going?'

'Would you come to my hotel?'

'I'd much rather have a drink somewhere.'

They went to a large café, some of the customers looking more tired even than the tired waiters. David ordered a bottle of champagne.

'I was over in England the other day,' Margery said. 'My mother's funeral, my first visit since thirty-eight. My four sisters were there, our first meeting since thirty-eight. They had become complete strangers. Have you noticed there is no bridge between different kind of lives?'

'I'm beginning to notice.'

'To survive I had to prostitute myself while two of my sisters were Wrens and the other two brought up their children. And I missed Paris badly, so I came back the day after the funeral. Another surprise awaited me. The man I called my protector was released from jug, we met, and I – who had been thinking of him and waiting for him – hadn't a spark of liking left for him.' She smiled at David. 'Whereas when you came into the bar I was aglow with pleasure.'

'I'm glad,' he said, taking her hand.

'Yet I knew you during my worst period. You want me to go to your hotel?'

'Nothing I want more.'

'You'll come to my flat. It isn't far from here.'

They left after finishing the champagne. Her flat was on the top floor of a building in the rue des Capucines. It was strikingly a woman's flat with lots of looking glasses, framed photographs and vases with faded flowers. 'Who are all those people?' David asked, pointing to three photographs in the same frame.

'Haven't the faintest idea,' said Margery. 'The flat belongs to some woman who used to be a regular customer at the bar. She's gone to Marseilles, where she has a rich lover, so she let the flat to me.'

She sat down in an armchair, crossed her long legs, then uncrossed them and rose. 'Let's go to bed,' she said. 'We can talk better in bed.'

Till eight in the morning they spent their time either talking or lovemaking. She declared that with no other man had she felt so at home, so at her ease. He assured her he was completely at ease with her. How long would he stay in Paris? He had come for a few days, yet would remain for a fortnight in order to be near her. At eight o'clock he got up, said he would go to his hotel to have a bath and a shave. She said she would sleep till mid-day, and they could meet in the bistrot downstairs. She turned up at half past twelve. He took her to lunch on the Left Bank.

For thirteen days his routine didn't change. He had no idea whether he was in love with Margery, but to be in her company was perfect bliss. He made friends with Mme Hermine who, the night before his departure, said, half in earnest, 'I hope you won't steal my Marge. She's the most useful assistant I ever had. Here one has to be as hard as nails. She's even harder.'

You don't know Margery at all, said David to himself, thinking of Margery's expression during the act of love, as soft as velvet. 'I won't steal her,' he said aloud. 'We've no plans whatever.'

He promised Margery he would be back in Paris in no time. He bought her a gold bracelet, and she saw him off at the Gare du Nord. He connected her no longer with the girl in Pigalle. On his arrival in London he found a long insulting letter from Victor. The best sentence, he thought, was, 'I gave you the chance to redeem yourself. You wilfully missed it.'

David kicked off the second shoe, then got into bed.

2

Elfrida lived in a snow-white block of flats in a two-room flat. Every flat in the house had two rooms. If you bought a flat there you could choose between light blue or pink walls. Elfrida had chosen light blue. The sitting-room overlooked the sea; every sitting-room overlooked the sea, which now and then looked as artificially blue as the blue walls. On the walls hung reproductions of paintings by Marquet and Vlaminck, the imitation Louis XV armchairs had blue seats. Elfrida was in a rotten mood at four in the afternoon, for if she hadn't asked Margery's son to tea she could be in Alice's London Bar chatting with and gazing at David. She made no secret, when alone, of her devouring passion for David. If she came home tipsy at night she pictured herself in his arms, and that was almost as good as the act itself, which she feared she wouldn't ever know. She was born to be his wife, and she saw herself and David living in true harmony between the blue walls, and getting nicely tiddly together in Alice's London Bar. She frowned because Alice's London Bar meant Margery. She couldn't make out what their exact relationship was. They seemed close, like an old married couple who had no surprises left for one another. She was aware of Michel's existence, so that ruled sex out, yet on the other hand their intimacy was based on a total mutual understanding and compromise which, she was certain, no man and woman could acquire without having been lovers.

She took from the table her late husband's photograph. He had been such a kind man; such a bore too. She wouldn't have deceived him if he hadn't been so clumsy. The strange, inexplicable thing was that after his death she remained faithful to him. No, faithful to David whom she had met as a widow of six months. She had fallen in love with him, and every night on leaving Margery's flat she was resolved to throw herself at him. However, she had no idea of how to set about it. She went as far as asking Margery what she would do if she wanted a man very much. 'Push him into bed,' said Margery. How to push David into bed? He didn't look pushable.

The telephone bell rang. Was it Claud to say he couldn't come? Then she could fly straight to Alice's London Bar. it was the hall porter to tell her that a M. Darnell was downstairs. 'Send him up,' said Elfrida in a faint voice.

'I'm so glad you found your way here,' she said after opening the door to Claud.

'It wasn't difficult,' he said.

'Sit down, I'll make tea at once.'

62

She went to the kitchen which had blue tiles, made tea, found a packet of biscuits. 'You have a very fine view,' said Claud, standing at the window.

'At times I find it depressing,' said Elfrida. 'Sit down, and tell me all about yourself.'

'There's little to tell,' said Claud. 'My life was perfect till my father died.'

'You were very fond of him?'

'I loved him, also I admired him enormously. He hadn't a fault.'

'You have your mother.'

'We don't see much of each other,' said Claud, reminding himself that Elfrida was a friend of hers. 'I'm stuck to the land, mother is a townswoman.'

'Very much so,' said Elfrida, wondering what to say next. 'You ought to marry. With your father gone you must feel very lonely on the land.'

'There's Lil the housekeeper, but she wants to go. I have a fiancée in a way.'

'What do you mean by in a way?'

'We're not officially engaged, but we plan to be. She and her mother are neighbours of ours.' He winced. 'I ought to say neighbours of mine.'

'Are you madly in love?'

'I couldn't say that. It's something quite different.'

'If it's something quite different then don't marry. I know what I'm speaking about. To get away from a tyrannical old mother I married a man who was forty years my senior. It was a cold comfort marriage. If you don't feel love bursting in you don't do it.'

'Ludmilla is so nice,' said Claud, and as he said that he was unable to conjure up her image. Ludmilla sounded like a name without a body, a name you read but without picturing the person.

'Niceness isn't enough. More tea?'

'Yes please.'

'What do you make of David Woodlow? He's a great friend of mine.'

63

'We lunched together in mother's flat.'

'He's the most intelligent and amusing man I ever met.'

'He seems very nice.'

'Nice must be your favourite word.'

'Sorry,' laughed Claud. 'I won't use it again. He told me that he and my father had been together in the Army during the war. I asked him why he never came to see us. He said because he seldom leaves Cannes. But he said he knew our place.'

Elfrida was at her wit's end. She couldn't think up any more subjects. Would it be impolite to say she had an engagement, so had to go out? Hang politeness.

'I don't want to sound rude,' she said, 'but when I asked you to tea I forgot I had a date in your mother's bar at five. I'll take you there in a taxi, and you'll have a drink with me to make up for rushing away.'

'I'm going to walk, but thank you all the same.'

'We'll go down together,' said Elfrida, then went to the bedroom to choose a dress that David might like. It was so irritating that he never noticed what she wore, yet he would criticise or praise Margery's clothes. She put on a blue dress that matched the walls.

She and Claud stood nose to nose in the lift, which reminded him of Modeste. With her he had been more at his ease. He regretted not having seen her when he went out in the morning. The aunt, he thought, looked cunning and terrifying.

'Take my advice,' said Elfrida as they crossed the hall, 'and don't marry in haste.'

'There's no question of it.'

'No successful marriage can come out of a lukewarm relationship. You really don't want a lift?'

'No thank you, I do want to walk. Thank you so much for the tea.'

He waited in the doorway till Elfrida's taxi came, opened the door for her, then went off, trusting to instinct to find his way back to the rue d'Antibes which he had already explored. Was his relationship with Ludmilla lukewarm? It was difficult to say since he could make no comparison. True he had been to bed with a girl, that was in Folkestone, a pick up in a pub, and the only memory he retained of their encounter was that she smelt of beer. For that girl he had felt nothing, for Ludmilla he had surely stronger feelings, otherwise he wouldn't contemplate marriage. His father had said, 'A wife is essential for a man who lives in the country.' A lot of wisdom in that, but why had his father been so keen on his embarking on a life without ups and downs? He considered himself slightly disloyal for questioning his father's plans for him. That brought him to Lil who had admitted that she loved his father. There had been no ups and downs in their relations. He would send Lil a postcard tonight.

'Monsieur!' He heard a voice, looked up, and saw a 2CV pulling up. Modeste sat at the wheel. 'Can I give you a lift back?'

'That's very kind of you,' said Claud, getting in beside her. 'Have you come a long way?'

As a matter of fact she had been visiting her child. She did that practically every day, but never said a word about it to her aunt, who guessed, of course, where she spent her free time. 'I was in Antibes. Do you know Antibes?'

'I don't know the Coast at all.'

'Thursday will be my day off,' Modeste said timidly. 'I could take you for a drive, to see the Corniche and Nice and Monte Carlo.'

'I'd love that, mademoiselle.'

'Please don't mention it in front of my aunt. She's very strict about the attitude to take vis-à-vis hotel guests.'

'What sort of attitude does she want you to take?'

'To look at them as paying machines, not as human beings. Yet she wants those machines to leave satisfied so that they return and start paying again.'

'I'm sure I'll be a satisfied machine,' laughed Claud.

She laughed with him, and for the first time he noticed her eyes. To notice them was to compare them with Ludmilla's. Modeste's eyes changed their expression with every word she uttered; Ludmilla's were steady. He ought to send a postcard to Ludmilla, too.

65

'My parents died when I was small,' said Modeste, and there was a veil over her eyes. 'My aunt took me in and brought me up.' The veil lifted. 'So I shouldn't say a word against her. I must have a very ungrateful disposition.'

'I'm sure you haven't.'

'If one isn't commercially minded it is almost impossible to understand those who are.'

'I'm not commercially minded either.'

'Are you a student?'

'I'm a farmer.'

'A fermier? That's not how I imagined them . . . I'll stop here, you get out, and when you go into the hotel don't mention you saw me or that I gave you a lift.'

'Count on me,' said Claud.

An old man with a white walrus moustache stood at the desk, chatting with Mme Romei. As Claud asked for his key the old man's piercing blue eyes bored into his. Claud blushed under their impact. 'You're English,' the old man fired at him. 'My name is Rudge. What's yours?'

'Darnell, Claud Darnell.'

'Any relation of Archy Darnell?'

'I don't think so.'

'He was a DC when I was PC, a good chap. Are you on holiday?'

'Yes, sir.'

'Cannes has changed a lot since my youth. Come into the writing-room. Nobody's ever in there. People don't write letters any more.'

Claud followed him into the writing-room unable to think up an excuse for bolting. 'Sit down,' said Rudge. Claud sat down beside a writing table, and Rudge seated himself so near that their knees nearly touched. 'I bet you've no idea what a PC is.'

The fierce blue eyes were full of menace. 'Police constable?' asked Claud tentatively.

'Police constable,' thundered Rudge. 'So you take me for a bobby. Do I look like a bobby? Do I?'

'No sir, I'm sorry.'

66

'The result of the liquidation of the Empire. I don't blame you. How could you know, you who live in these evil days. PC stands for Provincial Commissioner, I'm a retired provincial commissioner from Kenya Colony. Got me?'

'Yes indeed.'

'A provincial commissioner is a man of great power and responsibility. I had great power and responsibility. Power and responsibility have gone. We live in an age without power and nobody has a sense of responsibility left. I must seem an old fossil to you.' Claud shook his head. 'But take it from me that your life will never be like mine was. Will you ever rule a whole province? Answer me.'

'I'm sure I won't.'

'Oh, here you are.' Claud heard David's voice. 'Hullo, Rudge. So you two have met. Your mother sent me, Claud. Come along, we must go.'

Claud jumped up like one liberated. Rudge looked from one to the other, undecided as to who deserved his wrath. 'Excuse me, sir,' said Claud as he followed David. He saw Modeste behind the small desk, smiled at her, then he and David left the hotel.

'That man's the biggest bore I know,' said David. 'Keep away from him.'

'He was angry because I didn't know what PC stands for.'

'Why should you? Do you like looking at boats?'

'Very much so.'

'We'll go down to the harbour, and then we'll go to your mother.'

When Elfrida arrived at Alice's London Bar, David had asked her what became of Margery's son. Elfrida replied that he had gone back to the hotel. David went to the counter behind which Margery stood talking to Alfred. 'A word with you,' David said. Margery came round the bar.

'What is it?' she asked.

'If you ask your son out here don't leave him to his own devices. You ought to amuse him, look after him. You don't want him to die of boredom.'

'That sounds terribly funny coming from you,' laughed Margery.

'I don't see why.'

'I don't know how to amuse him. We're almost strangers really. Besides, I've got a job to do.' She lowered her voice. 'After all, you're not a very good parent either.'

'Don't say that even as a joke.'

'What do you want me to do with him? Take him to the cinema?'

'I'm going to the hotel, take him for a walk, and then you must give him dinner in your flat, and after dinner let him stay there as long as he wants. If he gets bored first, that's fine. The other way it isn't.'

'Anything for peace,' said Margery, and went back behind the bar.

'You're going out, David?' asked Elfrida.

David nodded, and went to save Claud from Rudge.

After they had looked at the harbour David and Claud walked slowly to Alice's London Bar. They had to step off the pavement to let a silent group of Japanese go by.

'I used to farm a little,' said David, 'in my long forgotten past. Tell me about your farm.'

'You said you knew our place.'

'In my long forgotten past.'

'It's mixed farming,' Claud began, and while he spoke David thought of that day when he had taken Victor to the house which Victor had now left to the young man at his side.

They stepped off the pavement to let another silent group of Japanese go by.

3

Lil decided to go to London to see Walter, who had left her letter unanswered. Was it the wrong letter to write to a man like Walter? She would find out. The night before she had wanted to ring Margery to ask how Claud was. She had checked herself, remembering her resolution to be gone before

Claud came back. In one of the many books she had read, and whose contents she had mostly forgotten, she had been struck by a description of wives in India being burned after their husbands' death. She wished the book weren't such a vague memory. They were surely burnt because their usefulness had ended. She had been at times more than a wife to Victor, yet that didn't bring about the status of widowhood. So she had no excuse to be burned in spite of her usefulness having come to an end. None-the-less, she was entitled to vanish. Claud must learn to look after himself. Would Ludmilla be the right companion for that? Before she went for good she had one duty to perform, namely to make sure that Claud never found out, and that was why she was going to London.

Driving to the station she saw Mrs Coke in the distance, standing in front of a rhododendron as if expecting it to fly away. On the station platform she saw Ludmilla, and she groaned inwardly, for travelling up with her was the last thing she wanted. 'Hullo,' said Ludmilla.

'I think it's going to rain,' said Lil.

'Have you heard from Claud?'

'I'd a postcard.'

'So had I. What did he say in yours?'

'He said he liked Cannes.'

'That's exactly what he said in mine. He could have been more original.'

'What can one say on a postcard?'

'Lots,' said Ludmilla, 'but I don't blame him. I'll wait for his letter.'

The train came in, and Lil was relieved to see Ludmilla getting into a first class carriage. In the second class compartment she travelled in, a man with a well trimmed black beard sat opposite her, and whenever she looked up he gave her a conquering smile. She was still attractive in spite of the two years of abstinence Father Turle had forced on her. However, she was free now, and contemplating her dark and empty freedom she asked herself whether she would ever want a man again. She shook her head before she could answer.

Victor had swept her off her feet without having to make the slightest effort. When she had started living with him she had banged the door on her past, locked it and thrown the key away. Even with him gone there was no door in front of her, and if there were she knew it would be locked.

'May I open the window?' asked the man with the beard.

'Do,' she said without looking up.

It had begun to rain, and the rain beat into the compartment.

'I'd better close it,' said the man.

She ignored him, and when next she looked up she saw Tower Bridge.

The taxi queue was long outside Charing Cross station. Ludmilla was slightly ahead of her. Was she the right wife for Claud? Victor had wanted it, so she had no right to criticise. 'I don't want any upheavals in the boy's life,' Victor had said repeatedly. 'With Ludmilla there couldn't be any.' One night he had confessed to her that he regretted his own life inasmuch as he hadn't asked for or planned it. Had he possessed a little income, just enough to be able to live without worry, he wouldn't have embarked on all that he had embarked on. 'In that case we wouldn't have met,' Lil said. He said that was true, kissed her, then fell asleep clinging to her. The queue moved forward.

She was the first to admit she couldn't judge Ludmilla, whose existence had been comfortable from birth. As had Claud's, and she couldn't resist a smile. Ludmilla got into a cab. There was now only one dwarf-like man left ahead of her, and after he had left no taxi came for ten long minutes. 'It's always like that,' she said to the policeman, who, having no idea what she meant, pretended not to hear her. At last she was off.

She alighted from the taxi in Shaftesbury Avenue, and entered a dismal house. Climbing the stairs she wondered what Walter looked like now. She hadn't seen him for five years. I must have my wits about me, she warned herself as she rang his bell. Walter opened the door in person. He had become almost indecently fat, and, having been thin in his youth, it was superimposed fat. If he were only to make an effort she was sure he could shake it off. 'Lil,' he said, 'what brings you here?'

'I wrote to you.'

'You did, but I thought it would be better to wait for your next move.'

'Then why ask what brought me here?'

'A form of welcoming speech. Sit down.'

The room opening off the landing served as his office. On the walls were the sort of posters you associate with travel agencies. Walter had nothing to do with travel agencies. The furniture consisted of a desk, a filing cabinet and two chairs. Lil could smell onions and bacon frying. Was he living with a woman?

'I'm all ears,' said Walter, seating himself behind the desk. 'I thought Victor was immortal.'

'He may be now.'

'But out of our grasp,' laughed Walter, 'so he isn't immortal for us. Did Marge come to the funeral?' Lil nodded. 'Where's the boy?'

'With her in the South of France.'

'I admire her maternal instinct. Tell me, what will you do Lil?'

'I didn't come here to talk about myself. In my hand-bag I've a cheque for two thousand pounds made out to you.'

'Cheques don't interest me. I'm bankrupt.'

'I could let you have the money in cash.'

'That's better, Lil.'

'You know the conditions.'

'The dead 'un makes conditions. That's a good one. When I served my little sentence . . .'

'That had nothing to do with us.'

'In a way it had. Marge and Victor corrupted me.'

'Was it difficult?'

'You're fun,' laughed Walter, showing his yellow teeth. 'Anyhow, they corrupted you too.'

'I was a call girl when they met me.'

'Pity I knew you only superficially at the time,' said Walter, leering. 'Still it's never too late to mend.'

'Those two thousand pounds,' said Lil, ignoring the last sentence. 'I've had them in my account for years. The idea was that if Victor died I should give them to you.'

'As a final payment?'

'He never said that. They're to thank you for your discretion all these years. But you're right when you call it a final payment, because there can't be any more dealings between you two.'

Walter stood up and leaned over the desk. How disgusting his double chin is, said Lil to herself.

'I shouldn't have called it final payment, Lil. I should have called it buying my silence. I knew Victor only too well. He had his code of honour. He said to himself, if I leave Walter two thousand quid he'll consider himself in honour bound never to go near the boy Claud, and never reveal the truth to him.' Lil nodded. 'Are there any other strings attached to the money?'

'None.'

'I thought there would be.'

'I don't follow you.'

'To find something for you to do. You won't stay with Claud, you don't want to take on the son after the father, you must do something, and I, the old friend with the right connections . . .' he gave her a wink. 'Or is Margery going to do something for you in France?'

Lil stood up, Walter straightened himself, and they faced each other like two fighting cocks.

'Understand, Walter, that after my years with Victor I could never return to that life. He gave me happiness, I admired him, and because of that admiration I couldn't earn my living on my back any more.'

'All right, Lil, no need to get flushed. So the only string is my silence. I was silent all these long years, admit it.'

She wanted to say, because you feared Victor, but she thought that unwise. 'I admit it, and that's why Victor didn't forget you.'

'What will Claud do?'

'He'll carry on.'

'I could make a bad joke but I won't,' laughed Walter, sitting down. She understood, and blushed with anger. 'How will you get me the cash?'

'My account is in a Dover bank, but I can go to the nearest London branch and they can ring through to Dover.'

'I wouldn't do that for such a large sum. Go back to your place, get the money in cash, and I'll come out in a few days. Haven't seen the house for eighteen years or so.'

'Come tomorrow.'

'I can't,' said Walter. 'I'm on to a good thing I mustn't miss. I'll ring you in a day or two. Where are you lunching? Lunch with me.'

'Impossible. I want to see an old friend, and then I'm going straight back. Don't wait with it too long, I mean come as soon as you can.' Claud might come back earlier than expected.

'For two thousand pounds I'd walk the whole way to Dover. Pity you can't lunch.'

'Ring me before you come so that I can collect the money.'

'You could still make a fortune with that figure of yours, Lil.'

'Why didn't you answer the letter?' she asked from the door.

'To be truthful I wanted to see you and see how the land lay.'

She went down the stairs, and out into the rain.

She was dissatisfied, thought that everything had gone wrong. And the irritating part of it was that she had no idea why she thought that everything had gone wrong. She had come up to give him the cheque, never to see him after that. Now she would have to meet him again, and the notion of his coming to the house where she had lived with Victor and Claud filled her with nausea.

She took the first train back to Dover.

Alone in the compartment she sat with eyes closed. Instead of sleeping she relived with such clarity, and in so many colours, the beginning of her life with Victor that she believed it was taking place in the compartment, she still in her seat but as an onlooker watching Victor and Lil falling in love with each other.

She was at the time in close contact with a Miss Hulbert who was, to put it nicely, a London associate of Margery's. Miss Hulbert was short, fair and a bully. All the other girls who came in answer to Miss Hulbert's telephone calls were Frenchwomen who had married Englishmen for a fee. Miss Hulbert clung to her only English call girl because she was in love with her. Victor and Margery didn't approve of Lil's working for Miss Hulbert, as their business in England was based on French girls. In order to find favour with Victor, that is to be able to keep Lil, Miss Hulbert invited him on a Sunday, their day of rest, to her own small flat in Marylebone Road, her plan being to leave him alone with Lil who had promised to use all her arts of seduction. Miss Hulbert was a keen observer who had guessed long ago that there was no love lost between Victor and his wife.

Victor arrived at half past four, and the three of them demurely took tea in the small sitting-room. When Miss Hulbert announced, as planned, that she had to absent herself for a little while, Lil knew that she had won her cause. She knew something else, too, namely that she had never seen such an attractive man before. And so distinguished, she thought as Victor smiled at her. She put her hand on his arm, and gazed at him steadily. 'Won't she come back?' Victor asked. Lil shook her head, too moved to speak. Victor stood up, she followed suit, and gazing at each other they both undressed.

'What a perfect body you have,' said Victor. She blushed with pleasure, lay down on the narrow sofa, her eyes imploring him to hurry to her.

She, the expert at the game, made love timidly as though it were fragile and rare. For him it was an awakening, and when they had got up from the sofa she said in an imploring voice, 'Don't let me lose you.'

'You won't,' he said.

74

He took her out to dinner, and then they went to a hotel to spend the night, in the course of which he told her about himself and Margery and Claud. 'Come and live with me on the condition that you'll love the boy.' She said she was sure she would, for his sake. Miss Hulbert was angry and disappointed, and rightly so since she had engineered the whole business simply because she didn't want to lose Lil, who would now be gone from her completely.

The train stopped in Dover. Lil walked out of the station in the wake of Ludmilla. Could that girl love as she had done?

4

Michel was dressing. Margery remained on the bed, her eyes following Michel's movements. I think, she said to herself, I've had my share of him. Catching her eye, Michel smiled at her and she returned his smile, having no inimical feelings. He was a pleasant man. She couldn't deny that he was a satisfactory lover, in fact she couldn't even explain why she had had enough of him. She stretched her long legs, yawned, then lit a cigarette. Michel was dressed.

'I've got something to tell you, ma grande,' he said, coming to the bed. 'I won't be able to see you for a few weeks. I promised my wife a trip to Italy, and she insists on our going before her pregnancy becomes too conspicuous. She's a vain woman. We're going early next week, and will be away for a fortnight. I'll send you postcards.'

'Don't bother, because I won't be here.'

'Where will you be?'

'In England,' she lied. 'I've got so much to fix up there.'

'Your poor husband's affairs?'

'My poor husband's affairs.'

'Ring me when you come back. If I come back before you I'll ring you at once.'

'A very sensible arrangement,' yawned Margery.

She jumped out of bed as he bent down to kiss her. Thus they nearly collided which made him laugh, the happy fellow he was. He threw her a kiss, turned back from the door to throw a second, then left, forgetting to close the door. Margery got into trousers, chose a purple shirt, and went barefooted into the drawing-room, where she lay down on the sofa. The shutters were closed, the room was in darkness, only a few blinding lines on the floor showed that the sun wished to storm its way in. It was Margery's afternoon off. She rang for Sylvie who came in, bent double.

'Go down to the bar, Sylvie, and ask Mme Formby to come up and have tea with me. She's there, I'm sure of that.'

'The stairs,' groaned Sylvie. Margery pretended not to hear. David believed that if her ills were ignored then she would stop feeling ill. Sylvie straightened herself and went down to the bar, where she found Elfrida seated alone at her usual table, disgruntled because David hadn't put in an appearance. 'I'm coming,' she said to Sylvie. On her way upstairs she asked Alfred to tell M. David, when he arrived, that she was with madame.

Entering the drawing-room she blinked several times. 'One can scarcely see in here,' she complained.

'You'll get accustomed to it,' said Margery.

'Have you seen your son?' asked Elfrida, sitting down in an armchair which had been pulled up so close to the sofa that there was almost no room for her legs. She could have pushed back the armchair, however such an effort was beyond Elfrida.

'Not yet,' said Margery.

'Didn't he lunch here?'

'Not today. I asked David to take him out to lunch. Let the poor devil see a bit of the Coast. I think they went to Nice.'

So that was why there was no David in the bar. 'How long is your son staying?'

'A few weeks. Depends.'

Sylvie brought in the tea things on an enormous tray which she put on the table beside the armchair and sofa. She opened one of the shutters a little, and the sun burst in, lighting up Margery's purple blouse.

What well-shaped breasts she has, thought Elfrida enviously.

'Pour out the tea,' said Margery. 'I'm aching all over.'

'Michel?' giggled Elfrida.

'Michel, but he won't make me ache much more. I've had my fill of him.'

'Who'll be the next one?'

'Don't know yet,' laughed Margery. 'Not knowing yet is so exciting. The best moments in a woman's life.'

'Where does David come in?' Elfrida asked, blushing scarlet. 'Sorry, but I just don't understand your relationship.'

'We're sitting comfortably on the tomb of our love.'

'So you did love each other? Forgive me for being inquisitive, Margery.'

'We loved each other very much, but that was long ago.'

'But you're still great friends.'

'Have you ever been to Auvergne?'

'Never. I only know the Coast in France.'

'In Auvergne you find plenty of extinct volcanoes. Those volcanoes were in noisy eruption for thousands of years. Now they're silent and burnt out. Mountains, I'm convinced, have a language of their own. If one extinct volcano speaks to another it speaks differently and uses different words from when it speaks to some ordinary mountain that had never burnt with it. David and I are such two extinct volcanoes. That's all, but it's a lot. Anyway, I won't come between you and David, Elfrida. Give me more tea.'

Elfrida stood up to pour out tea. Margery was lying back on the sofa, looking like abandonment itself. Elfrida imagined David on top of her, and jealousy made her hand tremble, and she poured some of the tea into the saucer. 'How clumsy I am,' she said. She wished she could see Margery naked to find out what David saw in her. Margery sat up to take the cup. Those breasts aren't so fine after all, Elfrida consoled herself.

'Was David your lover before or after your husband?' she asked.

'I won't tell you the story of my life,' laughed Margery.

'Sorry, I know I'm asking too many questions. Just one more. Did you care for your husband?'

'Ours was a mariage de convenance,' said Margery.

'Your son was devoted to him. He said so.'

'And my husband was devoted to him,' said Margery, hearing Victor saying, 'It was God's wish the boy should come to me.' When he had said that he choked with emotion. Margery couldn't help smiling, because Victor could choke with emotion at will.

'The door bell,' said Elfrida with shining eyes.

The eyes continued to shine as David and Claud came into the room.

'Hullo,' said David. 'We lunched in Nice, and I showed him eighteenth-century houses in the old town. Your son has an eye for architecture, Marge.'

'Yet he wants to bury himself in the country,' said Margery.

'It was my father's wish,' said Claud.

Margery tried to catch David's eye. He wasn't looking in her direction.

'Any drink going?' David asked.

'Get the pastis from the dining-room, Claud,' said Margery. 'The bottles are in the sideboard.'

Claud left soon after he had brought in the pastis. He walked fast towards the hotel in the hope of finding Modeste alone. Mr Woodlow, he mused, was a strange man in that he couldn't place him. What did he do with himself the whole day long? In fact you could ask what he did with himself the whole year round. He had put several questions to him during lunch, questions he answered without enlightening him. Yes, he had an estate in England, it was in Norfolk, but he went seldom near it. A house? A large one, which was let. With a large house like that why did he live in a hotel room? He preferred to live in a hotel room, easier in every respect. Then Mr Woodlow vouchsafed the information that he had started his life in the South of France by renting a manoir near

Mandelieu. However, he discovered that all he was doing was turning the squire into a chatelain, which in his eyes had no purpose. He left the manoir to take up his abode in the Hôtel Romei.

'I'd feel miserable and homesick if I lived away from our house and farm,' said Claud. 'Don't you ever feel homesick?'

'How could I?' said David, which Claud found most unsatisfactory.

He went into the hotel. Modeste was alone in the hall, and he forgot David.

'Thursday is approaching,' he said, stopping in front of the big desk.

'We'll have a long outing,' she said. 'I'm free at two, can come back in the evening any time I like. Next week all will change because the lady who comes on my day off will be on holiday. I'll be just able to get out for a couple of hours in the afternoon to see . . .' She stopped herself just in time. 'To see friends.'

'But I'll be able to come and chat with you.'

Modeste gave him a glance that made him blush. How could eyes be so eloquent? She wore a grey dress with a white collar, and her small breasts were easy to picture. He wondered whether if he were to touch them, she would slap his hand as Ludmilla was wont to do. Mme Romei loomed up, holding a heavily scented handkerchief to her nose. Down came her right hand, the handkerchief passed to the left hand, and she shook Claud's vigorously.

'Monsieur, I hope you're enjoying your stay with us.'

'Very much so, madame.'

'I know your mother a little. I admire her business sense. Her bar does very well indeed.' Following Claud's glance she discovered, as it were, the existence of her niece. 'Did you telephone the electrician, Modeste?'

'An hour ago, my aunt.'

'You told him I don't agree with his bill?'

'I made it clear to him.'

'Please give me my key,' said Claud.

'Here it is, monsieur,' said Modeste.

79

Upstairs in his room Claud sat down at the table, determined to write a letter to Ludmilla.

'My dear Ludmilla,' he began, and Modeste appeared before him with her eloquent eyes. Plenty of time to write to Ludmilla.

IV

1

'Why do you always refuse to come back to my flat for a snifter?' asked Elfrida as she and David came out of Alice's London Bar.

'It isn't refusing. It's simply the wrong hour.'

'Then come in the day time.'

'We meet here in the day time. Good night, Elfrida.'

The moon was up, and from a nearby nightclub rose the throbbing noise of dance music. On reaching the rue d'Antibes David perceived that he wasn't tired enough to take himself to bed. He went into an all-night café, where he sat down at a table far from the counter. This, he thought, looking round, is far less respectable than Marge's. More honest, he added. The girls were simple tarts with no nonsense about them, the men were pimps or drug pedlars. You knew where you stood with them. Margery's bar life, if that was the right expression, had always been genteel in a way. Already at Mme Hermine in Paris that genteelness had been remarkable.

'A fine à l'eau,' he said to the waiter, and his thoughts floated back to the bar near the Madeleine.

Margery had seen him off at the Gare du Nord, waving till the Golden Arrow was out of sight. She remained with him all the way to Victoria, and the next fortnight was a fight with himself, for he longed to go back to her though he knew he shouldn't. He wanted to be an MP, to rise high in politics, and he was perfectly aware that in such a career there could be no room for Margery. He returned to Paris.

He arrived on the bar's weekly closing day. Remembering her address in the rue des Capucines he hurried there with little hope of finding her in. She wasn't the sort that stayed at home on a day off. To his delight he heard footsteps approaching the door. As it was flung open he stepped back to have a better view of her, and he smiled because she was taller than he remembered her. He gazed at her, comparing the picture he had retained with the reality in front of him.

'Ce n'est pas vrai,' she exclaimed, opening her arms.

'I didn't expect to find you in,' David said a little shyly.

'Come in, my darling,' she said after hugging him in the doorway.

The flat looked untidy, and the bed wasn't made. She said her charwoman was ill; he suggested they went out to dine; but she shook her head, saying, 'Now that you're here we'll stay. Have a whisky while I make the bed.' When the bed was made the telephone bell rang. 'I bet it's Lou,' she said, lifting the receiver. He listened with no special interest, hardly understanding the gist of what she said, yet his mind retained her words, and there came a time when he was finally able to put two and two together.

'If you follow my advice,' Margery said before she rang off, 'you'll go down to Cannes. Annette will look after you . . . No, it's no good staying in Paris. I told you they noticed you. Anyway, Hermine won't let you in.

'Some women are fools,' said Margery. 'Why haven't you undressed?'

They lay down and made love. 'I love those long legs of yours,' he said afterwards. At ten o'clock they went out, had sandwiches and plenty of wine, at midnight they were back in bed, where they stayed till the morning.

'I'm going to say something, David,' she said towards dawn, 'that I never said to anybody before. I love you, truly I do.'

'You never said that to your protector?' he asked after they had made love again.

'Never. Protectors one respects but doesn't love. What about you, my darling?'

'Can't you feel it?'

'I want you to say it.'

'I love you,' he said, and as he said that he remembered their first night together when he had paid her as one pays any prostitute. He was annoyed with his memory. 'What are the plans for today?'

'I can remain with you till three in the afternoon, then I must start work at the bar.'

'Listen, Marge,' he said, sitting up in bed. 'There's no reason whatever for you to work in a bar. I won't be the first lover who wants to keep his mistress. I'll give you whatever you want.'

'You're sweet, but never again am I going to depend on a man. Once was enough. In my work with Hermine I make good money, learn a lot, and one day I'll have my own bar. Anyway, I can be with you after midnight again.'

'I wish you'd said yes.'

'I can love without pecuniary interest.'

'I love you,' he said. Much easier the second time.

When he started dressing she asked why he was in such a hurry. He was going to his hotel to bathe and shave. 'Why bother about a hotel, David? You can stay here when you're over here.'

'That won't do,' he said. 'I must have an address in Paris, where my solicitor and land agent can contact me.'

'How grand you are.'

'And I have an old aunt who lives in Neuilly. She knows I'm here.'

'I see your point. As long as you spend as much time as you can with your whore the whore will be quite happy.'

'You mustn't speak like that, my love.'

'I just want you to understand I've no social ambitions. Pigalle levelled me down. Still, be careful. A woman in love for the first time in her life can become extremely dangerous.'

'I'm not afraid.'

A little tart with fuzzy hair had sat down at David's table. She had a doll-like face and hazel eyes. 'Will you buy me a drink?' she asked in a strong Niçois accent.

'Have whatever you want,' said David, and returned to his thoughts.

His third morning with Margery was full of sunshine. Spring was establishing itself in Paris. After his shave and bath in his hotel he fetched her in a taxi, and they went to Saint-Germain-des-Prés to sit on the terrace of the Deux Magots.

'This is the sort of day when one wants to live and die in Paris,' he said.

'That won't stop you going back to your flat in Norfolk.'

'But I can come back. You'll tire of me before I tire of you.'

'I doubt that,' said Margery. 'See that man coming out of the church? Isn't he that friend of yours who was with you when I met you?'

'It's Victor Darnell all right,' said David, hoping Victor wouldn't notice them.

Victor crossed over, looking as handsome and distinguished as he had on the day he asked for David's Sussex house and farm, and came straight up to their table. 'Hullo, David,' he said. 'Didn't know you were in Paris.'

'I'd no idea you were.'

He introduced Victor to Margery, whom Victor didn't recognise. David's eyes signalled to Margery. She nodded. She's quick on the uptake, he thought. 'Sit down and have a drink, Victor. I'm afraid we must leave very soon.'

'In that case I'd better telephone right now,' said Margery, getting up and going indoors. Victor's eyes didn't even follow her.

'How are you and what are you doing?' David asked.

'I came over because some bloody fool thought there was a job going here with an English firm. He thought wrongly, tonight I'm going back. I'm glad to have run into you, David. Remember that trip to that house of yours near Dover?' David nodded. 'The offer I made you still stands.'

'What do you mean by an offer?' asked David, staring at him.

'My offer was that a rich man like you could give me that house and the farm that goes with it without feeling or suffering any loss. You refused. Your argument was that one doesn't give houses and farms away. A droll argument since my case wouldn't create a precedent. David Woodlow gave a house and a farm away, therefore everybody who has a house and a farm has to give them away.'

'Rather funny,' said David, trying to laugh.

'Not funny because it just isn't so. You can give them away without the slightest risk of other people following your example. But now I have an even better offer to make. You sell them to me, but I don't have to pay the purchase price. As simple as that. The whole world will think I paid for it, only you and I will know the truth, and I give you my word of honour I'll never divulge it to anybody. We can do the deal the day you come back to England.'

David was sure that his jaw had dropped and that he wouldn't find it again. Had Victor gone mad? Had the change from war to peace unbalanced the poor fellow?

'Victor,' he said gently, 'I can't give that house away. It was left to me by my father, and I have a responsibility towards it.'

'Letting it crumble, you call that responsibility. I could restore it beautifully. I fell for that house.'

'If you're hard up and need any money, say a hundred pounds or so . . .'

'I'm not a beggar,' said Victor, rising with great dignity. 'It's the house and the farm or nothing.'

'Wait for your drink.'

'I can't, but my offer still stands. If it involved the slightest sacrifice on your part I wouldn't make it.'

David watched him walk away, and couldn't help shrugging his shoulders.

'Your friend's gone?' asked Margery coming back.

'He's a bit weak in the head.'

'Anyway, he told me in that café in Pigalle that he'd never give money to a woman.'

In the afternoon David accompanied her to the bar, then stayed on for a drink. The first customer to open the door was a thickset man with a heavy moustache. 'I've come to see you, Mme Marge,' he said, 'about the Suzanne business.'

'We don't want to have anything to do with her,' said Margery.

'You and Mme Hermine think you rule the world,' said the man aggressively. 'I warn you, women can't play the fool with men. You'll hear from me.'

He stamped out of the bar. The telephone rang. Margery answered it, and her words remained engraved in David's memory again. Margery assured the caller that Julie would be at the bar towards seven.

'What did that man want?' David asked.

'Just wants to frighten us, but he's right in a way. A man is more feared than a woman. Now, my darling, leave me to my work, and be here before midnight.'

'I love you,' he said.

The little tart with fuzzy hair was drinking beer. Coming out of the past, David eyed her in bewilderment before recollecting that she had asked herself to the table. She looked contented with life.

'Do you never talk?' she asked.

'Not when I'm thinking.'

'I must talk to someone when I think. If alone I can't think at all. You're English?' David nodded. 'I'm from Nice but I have an English Christian name. Nelly. My mother says that's a typical English name. Are you on holiday?'

'I live here.'

'Will you take me to your house?'

'I live in a hotel.'

'Hotels can be very pleasant too. You won't be disappointed in me.' She swiftly touched him. 'I know you won't be.'

David thought that over. Of course it would end in disappointment, but she might give him a couple of hours without imposing her existence on him. He couldn't resist smiling, because the past alone had the power of imposing itself on him. 'Come to my hotel,' he said.

She trotted along at his side, telling the story of her life. Her mother was a nurse in a Nice hospital, and she herself was an apprentice hairdresser which only brought in a little. Therefore once or twice a week she came to Cannes to add a few francs to her income. She assured him she was choosy.

David gave the night porter a five-franc tip, took Nelly up

in the lift. And as they opened the lift door he saw Rudge, in a camel hair dressing-gown, emerging from the lavatory. Rudge glared at him. 'Hullo,' said David. Rudge tossed his head, then marched to his room on the other side of the landing.

'What a beautiful room this is,' said Nelly as David opened his door.

'Have a whisky.'

'I'll undress first.'

Nelly had big yet firm breasts, with nipples like oranges both in size and colour. 'How old are you?' David asked.

'Eighteen and a half.'

He was sure she was seventeen or sixteen. He should give her some money and tell her to go. She leaned over him, the breasts touched him, and his resolution was gone. When she left an hour later he congratulated himself on having forgotten to think in her presence.

2

Thursday brought with it a lot of sunshine and the mistral. Margery said at lunch that the mistral made her fidgety, and that she liked to see nobody when it blew. Taking the hint Claud didn't stay for lunch, and thus arrived punctually at the street corner where Modeste was to pick him up. She was two minutes late.

'I'm so sorry,' she said as he got in beside her, 'but my aunt insisted on my making out the bill for some people who are leaving only tomorrow morning. She's like that.'

'You're not happy with her,' said Claud.

'I can't say I am, yet she took me in after my mother died, so I'm not entitled to complain about her.'

'I was very happy with my father. He died the other day.'

'Poor monsieur.'

'Call me Claud.'

'Call me Modeste when my aunt isn't present. In front of her we can only be strangers. Do you know Nice?'

'I've been there with M. David.'

'Then we'll go straight to Villeneuve-Loubet, where I must see an acquaintance. But that won't take long. Then we'll go on to Monte Carlo.'

'Never been there,' said Claud, and they drove in silence. Now and then he glanced at her. Her profile he liked, the long dark eyelashes impressed him, and again he wondered whether she would behave like Ludmilla if he touched her breasts. Anyway, her breasts must be much smaller than Ludmilla's.

Modeste was thinking less of Claud than of what her aunt had said, as though guessing that she was meeting him. 'Alice's London Bar,' Mme Romei said, 'is a sort of discreet brothel, a refined one I should say. Our guest's mother carries it off beautifully. Still, it can't be much fun being that woman's son.' Modeste simply couldn't believe it. Claud looked too pure to be such a woman's son. Besides, M. David, whom she considered a grand seigneur in every sense, spent his afternoons and evenings in Alice's London Bar. She was certain that he wouldn't go near it if it really were the place her aunt called it. That reminded her of the night porter telling her, before he went off, that M. David had the other night brought in a girl who couldn't have been more than seventeen. Modeste sighed, for who was she to judge? A fallen, evil girl, her aunt had said when she discovered she was pregnant.

'You drive very well,' Claud said.

'You think so?'

'I don't think, I can see it.'

She smiled, and with the brutality shyness alone can give he pinched her arm.

'You hurt me,' she laughed.

'I'm sorry.'

'You don't have to be sorry,' she said, her hand touching his.

'I like you very much.'

'I fear I like you too.'

'Why say fear?'

'Because you're a bird of passage.'

'You must come some day to England to see my farm.'

'That's very problematic.'

'Not if you really want to.'

'You said that so nicely,' she said, but he didn't hear her because of an enormous lorry she was overtaking.

On reaching Villeneuve-Loubet she pulled up in front of a little house with a small garden. 'I won't be long,' she said. He remained seated in the car, taking no interest in the landscape dotted with pylons. He heard Modeste's voice, turned his head, and saw her with a baby in her arms, talking to a fat woman in a red skirt. It must be the fat woman's baby. He was too busy with his thoughts to take much notice of the baby. Why did he feel so differently about Modeste? Was that a sign of love, and if it was did it mean that what he felt for Ludmilla had nothing to do with love? How could he make sure that it wasn't just an ordinary infatuation that would leave him once he returned to Sussex and Ludmilla?

'Here I am,' said Modeste.

They drove on to Monte Carlo, and sauntered about in the mistral. He could hardly restrain himself from taking her hand. How did one lay siege to a French girl? Modeste wasn't the sort, he felt instinctively, that you could sweep off her feet in a fit of giggles. The beer-smelling girl came back to his memory. It had started with pinching and giggles, and ended with nothing to say to each other. At a street corner stood a young man and a girl in close embrace.

'May I offer you a drink?' Claud asked.

'I'd like a coffee,' said Modeste. 'We'll go back to the car and drive up to Monaco, where I know a quiet little café.'

In the car he touched her hand, and received the full warm blast of her eloquent eyes. The café was certainly a quiet little place with a wooden counter and three marble topped tables. An old woman with red-rimmed eyes served them, then sat down behind the counter. There was a fair number of flies about. Claud and Modeste sat side by side, his hand on her knee, his eyes averted as though the hand had no connection with him. But then hers covered his, a light and fresh hand, and throwing his shyness to the wind he bent over and kissed her. The woman behind the counter was concentrating on her knitting. As her mouth opened to let his tongue in he knew he had found the answer. He was in love and no nonsense about it. He touched her left breast, and felt the nipple harden under the dress. Ludmilla would have slapped his hand, whereas Modeste began to tremble all over. The next kiss was even better and deeper than the first.

'We ought to go back to the car,' Modeste said. 'Easier there.'

On reaching Cap d'Ail she turned off the main road, took a lane that was little frequented, pulled up near a clump of trees, and they kissed and necked in earnest. For the first time in his life Claud understood why the great lovers of history had been so reckless. 'You're wonderful,' sighed Modeste. 'I liked you the moment I saw you.'

'I'm in love with you.'

'You shouldn't be.'

'Why not?'

'I'll tell you some other time. I don't want to spoil our afternoon. Anyway, I must go back.'

'Just once more, Modeste.'

'How sweetly you say my name,' she said, then let him put his hand inside her dress and touch and caress her breasts.

When they drove off he sat in silence, unable to sort out his thoughts or explain to himself what he felt. She wasn't in a speaking mood either. Her student night porter had chaffed her for taking it seriously. Love was too flimsy for that, he repeatedly said. Now I'm taking it seriously again, she scolded herself, in fact far more seriously.

'So I'll have to wait for another week before we can be together again,' Claud said as they stopped in Cannes.

'I think we'll be able to manage to meet sooner,' she said. She pulled him over and kissed him, clinging to him. 'Claud,' she murmured.

Claud reached the hotel before her. Mme Romei sat behind the large desk, looking disgruntled. Though avid for money she preferred her niece doing the work for it.

'Your maman rang up,' she said. 'She wants you to ring her.'

'I'll call her from my room,' said Claud, taking his key.

'Claud,' said Margery on the telephone, 'I can't give you dinner tonight. I must go out, but come here all the same because David will give you dinner.'

Claud sat down at his table determined to write to Ludmilla. What could he say? I met a girl here who's not like you and that's why I like her? Ludmilla would snigger, show it to her mother who would declare it was high time for Claud to return, then mother and daughter would laugh their heads off. A postcard of Cannes Harbour or the Croisette was a simpler and easier proposition. He caught himself regretting he had ever known Ludmilla.

Modeste was behind the large desk, listening to an American hotel guest who wished to hire a car. Claud managed to give her a smile into which, he hoped, he had put all his sentiments. Her smile he carried away with him.

Alice's London Bar was pretty empty. The afternoon drinkers had mostly left, and it wasn't time yet for the night crowd. David and Elfrida sat with an angular woman whom Claud hadn't seen before. David waved to him.

'This is my sister Violet,' said Elfrida.

'A sister who has to put up with staying in a hotel,' said Violet.

'Don't start again,' said Elfrida. 'There's no room in my flat.' As a matter of fact there was, but if Violet stayed with her all hope of David going to her in a moment of weakness would evaporate. 'Anyhow, you're staying only a week.'

'I think I'll leave before,' said Violet.

'Young man,' said David, 'we're going. I'll take you to quite a good restaurant in Juan-les-Pins.'

'Couldn't we join you?' said Elfrida.

'I'm sure your sister and you have a lot to tell each other. Come, Claud.'

Elfrida looked with boundless hatred at her sister.

'How did you spend your day?' David asked as they left.

'I went to Monte Carlo.'

'The best musical of the century.'

Claud laughed, and David thought that the boy had a

happier disposition than he. Before Margery left she had told him about Lil and Victor having had no sexual relations the last two years of Victor's life. She considered that quaint and funny.

'I think it's admirable,' said David.

'There was nothing admirable about Victor,' said Margery.

'It's admirable to have faith, and the way he brought up Claud was admirable too.'

'In his stupid and vain fashion he persuaded himself that Claud was his son. I think I told you I never went to bed with Victor. How could I have? I was too deeply in love with you.'

David ignored the last sentence, too painful for words because what she said was true. He had been deeply in love with her, too, but they were not quits since he had put his ambition above her. Look where he was now.

'We'll take this taxi,' he said to Claud, and while they drove to Juan-les-Pins he mildly wondered what his life would have been like had he shaken off ambition as you shake off a cold. Could Margery have made the grade as the squire's wife after Pigalle and Hermine's bar? He had ruefully to admit that she would have made a success of it. All there was left to do was shrug his shoulders, which he frequently did.

'I want to ask you a question,' said Claud in the restaurant.

'Fire away.'

'What's the difference between infatuation and being in love?'

'Infatuation can end up as love, whereas love can't finish as infatuation. Is that a satisfactory answer?'

'Not really,' said Claud. 'I'm speaking about myself, as you surely guessed.' David nodded. 'I've met a girl who makes me feel as I never felt before, and that's why I can't place my feelings.'

'Is that the girl who lives near you and whom Margery tells me you're going to marry?'

'Oh no,' said Claud loudly. 'Not her at all. It's somebody I met very recently.'

'What do you feel about your neighbour?'

'We've known each other for ages. When we said we ought to marry in time it was because we've known each other such a long time. It's a friendly relationship like . . .'

'Like wanting to marry one's sister. I'd a sister whom I made swear she would marry me and nobody else. However, I was six at the time. At twenty-two one doesn't marry one's sister any more.'

'I begin to see you're right.'

'Better to follow one's feelings than stick to a mild brotherly relationship. I know what I'm talking about. You'll be happier with a slut if you're in love with her than with the finest paragon of virtue if your heart isn't engaged.'

3

Lil was getting impatient. Nearly a week had gone by since her London visit, yet not a word from Walter. What was he up to? Two thousand pounds was a tidy sum, and Walter wasn't the man to treat so much money lightly. He had gone to prison for far less. How still the house was, with her in it alone. The telephone bell broke into the stillness, Wilf barked, and she went to answer. To her great relief she recognised Walter's voice.

'I'm coming down at noon,' he said. 'Get the cash and give me a good lunch.'

She put down the receiver, and went to the garage. That garage Victor had built himself. What a wonderful man about the house he had been. If she compared the house with what it was like when she came to live in it she couldn't believe it was the same. She wiped her eyes, decided to take some flowers to Victor's grave in the afternoon, got into the car, and before she could let in the clutch she heard Ludmilla hailing her.

Ludmilla carried a straw basket that contained a detergent, soap flakes and two tins of sardines. She must have been to the grocer's.

'Look at this,' she said, waving a postcard.

It showed the harbour of Cannes. 'I am having a really excellent time. Love Claud.'

'What does he mean by an excellent time, Lil?'

'It means he's enjoying himself. Claud is so easily satisfied, he has a really happy disposition.'

'His life is here, not there.'

'Don't worry, he won't get stuck there.'

'You don't understand what I mean. His life and my life are attached to all this.' She made a sweeping gesture. 'Not to a sham world like Cannes. Mummy knows it and doesn't care for it.'

'Seeing a different world might do him a lot of good.'

'I disagree. I wish you'd found some excuse to get him back. I don't want him to become a sham like the place.'

'There'll never be anything sham about Claud. I must drive to Dover. A friend of Mr Darnell is coming down to lunch.'

'I repeat I don't like it. We must think up some excuse to get him back.'

'Why don't you go out and fetch him?'

The notion of her travelling to Cannes she found too ludicrous for words. She gave Lil the smile she reserved for Gretchen when her English got too exuberant. Shaking her head she said, 'Mother would be horrified if I suggested such a thing.'

Is it your mother or you who wants to marry Claud, Lil felt like asking. She made instead a quick gesture, which Ludmilla could interpret as she fancied, and drove off. When she put the two hundred ten-pound notes into her bag she felt as she was sure a miser would feel on parting with his treasure. Five hundred pounds was more than enough for a creature like Walter. As it was Victor's wish, she couldn't but give Walter the lot.

She was in the kitchen preparing lunch when the front door bell rang. Without waiting for her to let him in Walter opened the door, and since he knew his way about he went straight into the library, where she found him after she had looked for him on the porch. She flushed with anger. Damn it, the man wasn't in his own home.

'Dear Lil,' said Walter. 'Your dress suits you. Makes you absolutely charming. What will we have for lunch?'

'Chops.'

'Romney Marsh lamb, jolly good. What veg?'

'Peas from the garden.'

'Garden peas,' laughed Walter. 'Could I have a drink? My throat is parched.'

'There's a bottle of whisky in that cupboard, glasses too. Help yourself, I must go back to the kitchen.'

Wilf appeared, growled at Walter, then followed Lil into the kitchen.

'She's devilishly attractive,' said Walter to the room, as he fetched the bottle and a glass. 'No soda or water,' he mumbled and went to the kitchen, where Wilf growled at him again. Lil was bending over the table, her white blouse and skirt showing her shape, and he could feast his eyes on her left thigh, almost whiter than the skirt that had been caught up by the back of a chair. Lil straightened, and the skirt came down. 'What is it?' she asked.

'No water, no syphon.'

'There's a jug,' she said. 'We've no soda water left.'

'By "we" you mean Claud and you.'

'For me, "we" is still Victor and me.'

'How moving,' he laughed, taking the jug.

I must, said Lil to herself, try to be pleasant to him. I mustn't annoy him, as all I want is never to see him again. She put on a huge smile as she entered the library. 'Can I help you to whisky?' Walter asked.

'Yes, please,' she said, beaming on him. 'Before I drink I'm going to give you the money.'

'No special hurry,' said Walter.

She fetched her bag from the kitchen, counted out the two hundred ten-pound notes, then held them out. 'A nice little sum,' she couldn't help saying.

'Good old Victor,' said Walter.

'Don't ever forget why he left you this money,' she said in a pleading voice.

'Victor knew he could trust me. He can trust me in death

95

as he trusted me in life. Besides, what advantage would spilling the beans give me?'

'You could ruin an awfully decent young man's life.'

'Not my line. I like you in white, Lil.'

'Let's go and lunch,' she said, making for the door.

That was the first time the dining-room had been used since Victor's death. She saw herself, sitting with him and Claud when the three were alone, serving the meal if there were guests. She had indeed been the all-round woman for Victor : mistress, companion, governess, cook and parlour maid. Now I'm nothing, she sighed.

Walter talked away bothered by her silence. He praised himself, declaring that few men had the sensibility and understanding to match his. He was married, which Lil probably didn't know. 'There was a kitchen smell when I was in your office the other day,' Lil said. Walter thought that funny, laughed loud, then touched her arm. She pulled back and sat disconcertingly straight and aloof for the rest of the meal. However, you couldn't disconcert Walter.

'My wife,' he said, 'is no patch on you, Lil. Even her cooking isn't as good as yours. I often wonder why I married her. I suppose there are moments when one feels lonely. Loneliness is a very bad counsellor. Mind you, I can get rid of her when I want. She used to be one of Miss Hulbert's girls like you.'

'I've forgotten Miss Hulbert long ago.'

'She hasn't forgotten you. The other day she dined with us. I told her Victor was dead, and she asked what would become of you. I said I was coming here today. She sends her love. Tell me, was there anything between you two?' He leaned forward, leering at her.

'I told you I'd forgotten her long ago.'

'She certainly hasn't. She said she'd welcome you with open arms.'

'Tell her,' said Lil, rising from her chair, 'that under no condition will I go near her. Explain to her, if you think it necessary – I don't – that I ceased to be the person she knew when I came to live with Victor. I've absolutely nothing left in common with the Lil who existed before Victor.'

'I don't think that'll impress her. Victor was in business with her till he earned enough to pull out.'

'That has nothing to do with it,' said Lil sharply. 'That ceased thirteen years ago, and you're as aware as I am that once he finished with it he turned his back on it all. I remember you coming here ages ago, offering a good little business . . .'

' . . . a bar like the one Margery had in Paris.'

'What did Victor say?'

'He turned it down, he was even annoyed, but I was annoyed too. The way he spoke one could have believed he never had any truck with girls who earn a living.' He laughed loudly.

'He was strong enough to forget the past.'

'That's rather cute, Lil. I wish I'd a woman who stood up for me as you stand up for him.' He frowned. 'I don't really wish it. I'm honest with myself, so nobody needs to stand up for me.'

'I'll bring the coffee to the library,' said Lil, opening the door for him.

He couldn't resist touching her bosom as he went past her. She stepped back and looked away. Let him go soon, she prayed.

Walter paced the library briskly. He had retained the movements of the thin man he had been, in fact he often forgot his present bulk, and would knock into people in the street. 'Sorry, I miscalculated,' he once said to an angry old woman he had nearly knocked over. When Lil appeared he put out his cigarette, though it was only half smoked. He waited till she had put the tray on the round table in the middle of the room, then bounced forward and threw his arms round her. 'Don't,' she cried, trying to wriggle out of his embrace. She couldn't because of his weight and strength. He pushed her to the sofa and, with his arms gripping her, his weight alone sufficed to throw her on the sofa. He landed on top of her.

'There's nothing I want more,' he panted.

'You pig,' Lil shrieked.

She was pinned down by his body, so he could use his hands. The right hand fumbled with the buttons of the blouse, while the left worked its way up under the skirt. Lil shrieked again. 'You'll shriek differently in a mo', Lil,' he said. 'You'll never think of Victor after me.'

Lil's third shriek was heard by Wilf who, after sniffing round the garden in search of new smells, was approaching the house. He burst in through the open french window. Walter saw the dog, the hand that had been working away under the skirt came up in self-defence, and was bitten hard by Wilf. Next, Walter thought, would be his face. He jumped up and Wilf bit his leg, for which he received a hard kick that made him reel. Before he could recover, Walter's hands were in an iron grip round his throat. By then Lil was on her feet, shouting, 'Stop it, Wilf.' Then she saw Walter strangling the dog. She pushed him away, and dragged Wilf by the collar to the kitchen, saying, 'Wonderful Wilf, what a faithful hound you are.' She locked him up in the kitchen. She pulled down her skirt, buttoned her blouse, and then, warning herself not to lose her temper, she went back to the library.

'That fucking dog tore my trousers,' said Walter, 'and look at my hand.'

'Go to the cloakroom, there's everything you need.'

'Don't you speak to me like that,' said Walter. 'It's all your fault.'

'Go and attend to your hand,' Lil said.

'You come with me. The least you can do is bandage my hand.'

While she washed and disinfected his hand, Walter observed he could sue her for damages. 'Don't make me laugh,' she said.

'Get a chair. I must sit down when you clean my leg wound.'

Lil brought a chair, cleaned and bandaged the leg wound, and then went to the porch, waiting for him to be gone. Wilf was barking frantically in the kitchen. My poor champion, she thought, it won't be long. For dinner she would give him the rump steak she had bought herself. Walter appeared, limping exaggeratedly.

'There's only one way you can apologise. Take me up to your room.'

'Haven't I made it clear that I don't want it? No man exists after Victor.'

'You weren't so difficult when you used to let any man do it for a fiver. I'll give you a fiver, just like old times, eh?'

'Not even for the two thousand pounds.'

'Then do it in memory of Victor. I'm as good at it as he was, if not better.'

'Don't insult his memory. Please go. You have the two thousand, so I repeat, go.'

She held the door open, and as he went out Walter said, 'All you whores are a lot of trash.'

She badly wanted to hit him, but refrained, reminding herself it would be unwise to make an enemy of him. After Walter had driven off she regretted that she hadn't. He carried in his pocket the price of his silence, so she could risk his enmity. Moreover, she would soon be out of the lives of all of them. She shed a tear, thinking of Claud whom she would miss for the rest of her existence. None the less, go she must. 'My wonderful, marvellous Wilf,' she said, opening the kitchen door.

4

Mme Hermine lived in well-earned peace and comfort in Super-Cannes. As though to recapture the atmosphere of the Nantes brothel, everything in her villa was silk, plush and gold. The ormulu of her empire furniture shone, the carpets were thick, marble and bronze Cupids abounded, and on the walls hung paintings of nudes. She was seated in a red silk-covered bergère, fat as a happy sow, her swollen feet resting on a plush-covered pouf, beside her a bottle of champagne on a console table, opposite her Margery whom she was entertaining to dinner, hence David taking out Claud.

'You ought to buy yourself a little home like mine,' said Mme Hermine.

'I'm content with my flat,' said Margery.

'Is one ever contented, ma grande Marge?'

'Materially speaking I'm contented, but with nothing else.'

Mme Hermine glanced round her drawing-room and sighed comfortably before observing, 'I'm contented in every sense.'

'Then why did you ask is one ever contented?'

'A manner of speech with me,' said Mme Hermine. She sipped a little champagne before she continued. 'I'm contented because I've no aspirations left. Now and then I see some handsome young man with whom I wouldn't mind going to bed, but then I remember I'd have to pay him. I didn't earn my little fortune to spend it on love. So I turn my head away, however alluring he looks, and I'm contented with myself for having the strength to say no.'

'You may have missed a jolly good romp.'

'When one reaches my age one can afford to miss a jolly good romp. On my seventy-fourth birthday I said to myself, No more follies, Hermine. I kept to it.'

'I've got to wait,' smiled Margery.

The maid pushed in an enormous trolley which she left beside the bergère.

'Lobster, ham of Bayonne, and a truffle salad,' said Mme Hermine. 'We'll finish with an ordinary mousse au chocolat. My cook makes it so well.'

Mme Hermine concentrated on the cold lobster, every mouthful covered in mayonnaise. The ham she ate without bread, because she didn't want to get any fatter, the truffle salad she enjoyed, and the mousse made up twice over in calories for the bread she had denied herself. After coffee and armagnac she became loquacious.

'How's M. David?' she asked.

'Very well,' said Margery.'

'I, who am an expert of the human heart, just can't understand why you two don't get together again.'

'Too much has happened to make that possible.'

'Yet you see each other every day.'

'That's the best.'

'What do you mean, dear child?'

'It's the best because we can't long for each other.'

'That's too deep for me. Be an angel and pour me out a little armagnac. Frankly, I don't understand.'

'Yet it's so simple. If we didn't see each other daily we might miss each other, and if one misses a person one invests him with qualities that nearness automatically kills. While David and I remain close to one another there is no fear of inventing qualities. In brief, we know where we stand. Once he went back to England for a fortnight. Luckily it wasn't any longer. I was beginning to think I was in love with him again.'

'You still are, dear child.'

'I know that, but while I see him I don't have to remind myself of it. For him I was, and remain, the dirty trick he thinks fate played him.'

'How right I was,' said Mme Hermine, stretching her thick arms in lazy content, 'when I warned you that in our profession one can't afford to fall in love. You didn't believe me.'

'You're wrong there,' said Margery, 'I knew I couldn't afford it, but love was too strong to listen to reason. An alcoholic drinks even when he can't afford it.'

'You should have forced him to marry you when you were going to have your child.'

'At the time he was getting married to a woman whom he hadn't bought for a thousand old francs in Pigalle.'

'Look how it ended.'

'The trouble is that it'll never end,' said Margery, rising. 'I must go back to the bar.'

'Ring the bell, and my chauffeur will drive you down.'

On her way to Alice's London Bar, Margery wished that Mme Hermine hadn't broached the one subject she preferred to forget. For she would never know, however hard and often she thought of it, whether she or David had behaved worst. At times she was certain it was him, at other times she took the whole blame on herself. The joke was that, had they met in her mother's house, the obstacles wouldn't have existed. She couldn't help smiling. Had she remained at home, the decent maiden, David wouldn't have looked at her. Their real basis had been the night in Pigalle.

Alice's London Bar was crowded. At the corner table sat David, Elfrida, her sister Violet and Claud. What did she feel about her son? Whenever she asked herself that question she tried to answer it truthfully. If she said : He is my son, therefore I love him, she knew she was lying. If she thought : I couldn't care less about him, she was conscious of that being a lie too. He was amiable, lived outside her orbit, so why ask questions? She waved to them, and went behind the bar.

'Margery is back,' said Elfrida.

'What I don't understand,' said Violet, 'is how a well-bred woman like her can keep a bar that's open most of the night.'

'One doesn't discuss a mother in front of her son,' snapped Elfrida.

'Don't bother about me,' said Claud, 'as I'm going right now. I only waited for mother to come back.'

Elfrida watched Claud stopping at the bar, exchanging a few words with his mother, then leaving. She turned to her sister. 'You chased him away.'

'I don't know what's wrong with you,' said Violet. 'You weren't like this at home.'

'I'm learning to live,' said Elfrida.

'I'm going for a stroll,' said David, getting up.

'You chased him away too,' said Elfrida.

'You're a completely changed creature,' said Violet. 'It must be Mrs Darnell's influence.'

'She's the best influence I ever had,' said Elfrida, her eyes on David chatting with Margery. Doubt and jealousy burned within her, adding a second layer of crimson to her flushed cheeks. Was Margery leading her up the garden? Were they still lovers, and all that boloney about extinct volcanoes just a lot of crap? 'I'm going to the bar. You don't have to come with me.'

'I'm going back to the hotel,' Violet said.

'I don't mind where you go,' said Elfrida.

On Margery's advice, Elfrida had booked Violet a room in the Hôtel Romei, which she had thought cunning on her part, for when calling on her sister she could knock on David's door, saying, Hullo, I'm on my way to my sister, can I see your room? He couldn't answer, No, don't come in. He was too well bred to be rude to a woman. It had misfired, however, because of her dense, unimaginative sister. After meeting David, Violet had asked who he was and what he did. Elfrida explained that he had been an MP, that his wife had died, that he had lost his seat, and had then thrown everything up and came to live in Cannes. 'So he does nothing,' said Violet. 'I despise men who do nothing, just a parasite.' Furious, Elfrida pointed out that David was a man of means, and therefore couldn't be a parasite. He had some great secret sorrow, and in her opinion a great secret sorrow entitled you to step aside. 'Bosh,' said Violet. From that moment Elfrida loathed and hated her sister, wishing she hadn't come. She wouldn't visit her in her hotel even though David lived there.

'I prefer to be with you two at the bar,' she said to David and Margery.

'Good night,' called Violet to them.

Elfrida pretended not to hear her.

'You two don't seem to hit it off,' said Margery.

'We got on fine in England, but Cannes isn't for her.'

'Is Cannes for anybody?' said David. 'I won't come to the flat tonight, Marge. I've decided to go to bed early.'

'I want to go to bed early, too,' said Elfrida.

She and David left simultaneously. He stopped in the door-way to say good night to her, but with the cunning that desire and love give she asked him to accompany her as far as the station, where she was sure to find a cab. 'You read so much in the papers about lone women being attacked at night. Nobody would dare to with you at my side.'

'All right,' he said unenthusiastically, and as the station came into view he pointed at the line of taxis. 'Now you're all right. Good night.'

'Wouldn't you care to come for a little nightcap, David? The taxi can bring you back.'

'You're too kind, but I'm going straight to bed.'

What does that woman want from me, he asked himself, hurrying away. He knew perfectly well what she wanted, had known it for a long while, yet it gave him a sense of distance from her by treating it as a question. Anyway, little, unimportant Nelly with her orange nipples was preferable to Elfrida.

He swiftly forgot her, remembering Margery's words before she joined them at the bar. Whenever she went to see Mme Hermine she returned as though she had a hangover. 'Looking at her is enough to bring it all back.'

'Stop seeing her.'

'She's the best friend I ever had,' said Margery. 'You know that as well as I do.'

Admittedly he knew that as well as she, and slowing down he thought of a weekend he and Margery had spent together in Dieppe, four months before he met Jessica. They arrived on Saturday at noon and went straight to the hotel where they fell into bed, forgot to lunch and felt no pangs of hunger when they got up at six to have a look at the sea. They dined on mussels and mackerel in a small restaurant near the harbour, and at ten o'clock were back in bed. 'No two people have ever loved like this,' said Margery before he switched the light off. In the morning they had no desire to rise.

'I've got to take the afternoon train back,' she said, lying on her back, the sun that had entered the room forcing her to close her eyes.

With all the years between, and with all that those years brought or forgot to bring, he still saw her with her eyes closed and her long body in repose, the sun picking out her breasts, then moving down like a lover. 'I don't want you to go back, my darling,' he said.

'Mme Hermine is expecting me. I never let her down. Besides, we've a very interesting bit of business on.'

'Business? What sort of business?'

'My poor darling,' she said, opening her eyes, 'you're an innocent. Do you think Hermine and I earn our living just by pushing drinks across the counter? I really thought you noticed that the bar is a discreet brothel.'

'A brothel?' he said, sitting up. 'They don't exist in France any more.'

'Call it a meeting place. We don't have to harp on words. Gentlemen want women, we find the women, that is to say we've got women up our sleeves. There's a hotel not far away that gives us a rake-off when we send a couple to them. Some of those women are in debt to Hermine, so we've got the upper hand. The other day we sent one who owes Hermine money to a similar bar in Monte Carlo, a little different from ours because there are bedrooms above, and the bar-keeper will deduct the debt with interest from her earnings, and send the money to Hermine. The business tonight is connected with two girls who have been sent to us from Lyons, carrying a nice load of debts on their backs.'

'But this is white slave traffic,' David exclaimed in disgust.

'Call it any name you want, darling,' said Margery, stretching her legs. 'They're not slaves, they like that sort of life, nobody forced them into it, they do it because it suits their temperament.'

'You must give it up at once. I've told you I'm ready to keep you.'

'David my love, I don't want to depend on any man. Not even on you. I earn a good living, can put money aside and so remain independent. If you don't like it don't think of it. Believe me, I feel surer of myself now than in my Pigalle days. Look where the sun has got to.'

It had reached her pubic hairs, lighting them up, and he, as if under the influence of the sun, fell on top of her. 'This alone matters,' she cried.

It was no good, said David to himself, pretending or thinking that the rot set in on that morning in Dieppe. He was too much in love to feel the disgust a man of his upbringing should have felt. They returned together to Paris, and he continued to go to Hermine's bar to take her back at midnight. He ignored what went on, and forced himself to forget the words she had uttered while the sun played with her body.

He went past the all-night bar where he had met Nelly. As though struck by a sudden revelation he retraced his steps and entered the bar. It was like the other night, the same customers, the same women, and naturally Nelly among them. She saw him, came up to him, and craned her neck, expecting a kiss.

'Come to my hotel,' David said.

'We must have a drink first, the patronne would be annoyed if we don't.'

'I appreciate that,' said David.

He had a whisky, she a glass of beer, and when they started for the hotel Nelly took his arm. 'I don't like that,' he said. She seemed to pout. 'I'm too old for it, my dear.'

'My father and mother are much older than you, but when they go out they walk arm in arm.'

'They must be less shy than I.'

Nelly laughed, said she had seldom seen a man less shy then he, and her mood was restored. On reaching the hotel, through the glass door he saw Claud talking to the night porter.

'I'm sorry, Nelly, but it won't be tonight.'

'What do you mean?' she asked harshly.

'It'd take too long to explain, but you can't come in with me. Here's a hundred francs, and I'll come and see you in a day or two.'

'I won't be fobbed off with money. I came because I liked you the other night.'

'I'm terribly sorry, but it can't be done. There's somebody in there, I don't want him to see me in your company.'

'Have you a wife then?'

'No, no, have another fifty. Good night, and we'll meet soon.'

'You're a monster,' she said, then went off, her head bent, defiance in her gait.

'Still up, Claud?' said David, pulling the door open.

'I was just going to bed.'

'I'm going too. Coming up with me?'

Claud wished the night porter good night, then travelled up in the lift with David who asked him whether he had found out the difference between infatuation and love.

'I'm beginning to find out.'

'Good,' said David.

They parted on the landing, each going to his room. David sat down on his bed, then got up and poured a fair amount of whisky into a glass, wishing Claud hadn't been in the hall. To be reminded of the past was for Margery the same as a hangover; he was having a hangover, too; Nelly in his bed might have chased it away. What was Margery doing with hers?

As a matter of fact Margery was climbing the stairs to her flat, accompanied by a young man she had noticed in the bar on several occasions. He had wavy black hair, a pointed beard and the whitest teeth she had ever seen. All she knew about him was that he was a journalist, working for a newspaper in Marseilles. He was on holiday, staying with a relation in Nice. 'Would you care for a drink in my flat?' she had asked him, looking straight into his eyes.

'How could a son of the Midi say no to that?' he said with an expression she found brazen. Anyhow, he understood what she wanted from him.

'Stay here,' she said in the drawing-room. 'My maid's gone to bed, I'll get you a drink. What's your Christian name?'

'Anatole. I don't care for it. Anatole Berry.'

'I don't need your family name.'

First she went to her bedroom to undress, putting on a transparent dressing gown, then fetched brandy from the dining-room. On entering the drawing-room she stopped under the chandelier, and in the strong light of the many bulbs she stood, waiting for Anatole to move. She didn't have to wait. He came to her with the dash of his youth and the Midi.

'Let me put the tray down,' she said.

'Take that off,' he said when she had done so.

'Undress. I hate to be touched by a person who's dressed.'

She watched him calmly while he undressed. As hairy as I expected, she said to herself. 'We'll start straight on the sofa, Anatole. I don't need preliminaries.'

'You're magnificent,' he mumbled.

He made love as if penetrating her were an answer to everything. The sofa shook, and Margery was certain she would wake up in the morning aching all over. And he was insatiable. The perfect anonymous fuck, she couldn't help thinking. His ardour abated towards three o'clock.

'You ought to go now,' she said, lighting a cigarette, her eyes on him but without any affection in them.

'Can I see you in the afternoon?' Anatole asked.

'In the bar. I don't want you to expect this to have a future. When you go out through the door I shall have already forgotten it, but thank you all the same.' He looked at her pleadingly. 'If you remind me even with a glance or a gesture I won't let you into the bar again. You seem intelligent enough to understand that this was the whim of a moment only.'

To show he was intelligent enough Anatole bowed, and left the room without looking back.

My hangover is cured, said Margery to herself as she lay down in her bed.

V

The night porter had been of no help, or was he, Claud, too clumsy to find out what he wanted? Mlle Modeste had changed rooms some time ago, and he, the night porter, wasn't certain to which room she had moved. He usually left before Mlle Modeste came down. Mme Romei, an early riser, was the one to whom he handed over in the morning. With that, Claud thought, he wouldn't get far. Since their glorious outing he had seen her to speak to only twice, on both occasions in her aunt's presence. Had she come to regret their kisses? He was the most miserable creature on earth.

He went down at nine to have his breakfast. Mme Romei sat behind the large desk, chatting with a woman in black, both speaking in Niçois. Mme Romei gave him the smile all hotel guests who paid their bill regularly were entitled to. No Modeste, and he went into the writing-room, which served as breakfast-room in the mornings. Few guests were present, since most of them took breakfast in their bedrooms. Rudge sat at one of the tables, so Claud chose one at which he could sit with his back to him.

Suddenly he heard Modeste's voice in the hall. He had left the door open on purpose. Then to his delight he saw her coming in. She wore the dress she had worn on their outing.

'A postcard for you, monsieur,' she said, and in giving it her hand touched his. 'She's going out in half an hour,' she whispered.

Claud nodded, she returned to the hall, and he decided to linger over his coffee and two croissants for half an hour. He nearly jumped as a heavy hand came down on his shoulder. He looked up : Rudge was glaring at him.

'Still here?' said Rudge.

'I'm still here.'

'You shouldn't be.'

'What do you mean, sir?'

'A young man like you shouldn't be in the South of France. It's all right for a retired high official like me, but not for a young man. I've done my duty, I can relax, but at your age you've no right to relax. The Riviera is bad for the young. Makes 'em idle. If you stay on you'll become a useless lounge lizard.'

To Claud's horror Rudge sat down at his table, saying, 'I'll tell you about my own youth, and let it be an example to you. When I was your age I was already shouldering my responsibilities to King and Empire.'

'Excuse me, sir, I must leave, my mother is expecting me. Perhaps some other time.'

'You forgot the postcard,' Rudge bellowed as Claud started for the door.

Claud took it, thanked him, and looking at the postcard he had to admit that he had glanced at it and had recognised Ludmilla's handwriting. He put it in his pocket, having no wish to read it in front of Modeste. Mme Romei was still chatting with the woman in black. Claud went out, stopped at the street corner, and read, 'I want a long letter from you. When are you coming back? Lots of love, Ludmilla.' The postcard showed Dover Harbour. One harbour in response to the other, Claud smiled. Turning round he saw Mme Romei coming out of the hotel in the company of the woman in black. They went off in the opposite direction. Claud waited a couple of minutes, then dashed back to the hotel.

'Modeste,' he said in a voice louder than he had intended.

'Claud,' she said.

'I never see you.'

'This afternoon I'm going to Villeneuve-Loubet, just going and coming back, no time to stop on the way. If you want to come with me be at the same corner at three. I'll pick you up.'

'Of course I'll be there.'

'How sweetly you said that,' she said, her eloquent eyes shining.

'Hullo, sir,' said Claud to David who had stepped out of the lift.

'I got up too early,' said David. 'I don't know why. Bonjour, Modeste.'

'Bonjour, monsieur,' said Modeste, her eyes still on Claud.

'If you haven't anything to do,' said David, 'come with me to that café at the corner. I always breakfast there.'

He shuddered as they came out, repeating that it was too early for him. He scarcely spoke while he breakfasted, which Claud didn't mind since he was thinking of Modeste whom he found even more alluring than he had thought her in the night filled with his longing for her.

'I'll see you at your mother's around one,' David said.

'I was going to ring up to say I can't come.'

'Why not?'

'I want to have another look at Nice. Anyway, I'll come to the bar in the evening.'

'Nice is worth a second look,' said David, thinking there wasn't much love lost between mother and son. 'It's more lively than lunching in a gloomy room with the shutters closed.'

Claud gave him a conspiratorial look, and they parted outside the café.

David sauntered to the Croisette, asking himself why he hadn't managed to stay in bed till eleven. Was it still the hangover? He ought to be immune to hangovers with such a vast experience of them. He sat down on a café terrace, asked for a pastis, then closed his eyes the better to conjure up Jessica.

He had come back from Paris and Margery, wishing he had remained, and motored down to Brinworth Hall, his residence in Norfolk. Frankly, he hadn't felt at home in it since his father's death. His father had filled the house, and once his father had gone it was too large, hence empty. Every room suggested the void. These houses, he often thought, weren't made for his generation, it was like lying in too big a coffin. The old butler who would retire at the end of the year told him that Mr Durie had telephoned the night before, and would Mr David ring him when he arrived.

'I thought you'd be back earlier,' said Lionel Durie who was a distant cousin of his. 'I'm giving a little dinner party tonight. Is it too late to ask you?'

'It's never too late. What time?'

'Towards eight, black tie.'

David arrived at eight; at eight-five he was introduced to Jessica.

David crossed his legs, asked for another pastis, shifted in his seat to escape the full blast of the sun, then returned to his reverie.

Durie's house was as large as his. However, Durie was twelve years older than he and had a wife and three children. David was put beside Jessica at dinner. At the port stage he was already resolved to marry her, yes, resolved, his passionate love for Margery notwithstanding. Looking back on that evening and on all that followed, he couldn't, however hard he tried, understand how he had expected everything to be plain sailing, knowing that his heart belonged to Margery. When one is young one has courage, and cheek was his excuse in retrospect. Aplomb, the French called it. His lucid mind deserved part of the blame. Why blame? He had calculated correctly, and it wasn't his fault that leukaemia would blow up the lot.

Jessica was attractive, had carriage and was friendly and intelligent, in short, the ideal wife for the future MP. Over the port Durie gave him the full dope about her. Her late father had been an MP, as had his own, an uncle of hers, too, and another uncle who was still alive had been under-secretary of state, and was an influential member of the Conservative Party.

Durie, who knew of David's ambition, said before they rose to join the ladies, 'She's made to be your wife. I could see she liked you.'

David had seen that too.

Jessica lived with her widowed mother in a manor a dozen miles away. He called on her two days later. Her mother was a woman who knew how to efface herself. Left alone with

Jessica he spoke of his plans, and she immediately suggested he meet her uncle Roger who could pull strings on his behalf, that is, find him a constituency if he took to him. 'I'm sure he will,' she said. 'You're quite irresistible.'

'Let's see,' he said, pulled her to him and kissed her.

The strange side of the kiss was that he enjoyed it, and made no comparison with Margery's. Jessica's mother kept him to dinner, and sitting opposite Jessica he studied her as you study some object you have a good mind to buy. Her grey eyes oozed honesty, her nose was long, her mouth intelligently large. While they had kissed he had felt her breasts which he was sure were firm. He had noticed on arrival at the Durie's that she had fine legs and ankles. There was nothing wrong or ungainly about her. Moreover, she knew about politics, talked politics, her manners were faultless, and she was vivacious enough not to become a bore. He would be a damned fool if he missed such a good catch.

'Your daughter,' he said to the mother before he left, 'has bowled me over. If I weren't bashful I'd propose to her right now.'

'Don't be bashful,' said the mother, giving him the encouraging smile he had hoped for.

He asked her to marry him while she accompanied him to his car.

'Should I say it's too sudden?' she laughed.

She got into the car with him, they kissed and hugged, and he drove away satisfied with the firmness of her breasts. That night he dreamt of Margery. They were making love in a field full of poppies.

Three days later Jessica took him to her uncle, that pillar of the Conservative Party who assured him that at the next by-election he would bear him in mind. 'Anyway, feeling is beginning to run against Labour.' The year was 1947. He and Jessica decided to marry in two months' time. 'Ours will be the perfect marriage, as we've the same tastes and interests,' she said.

'Hear, hear,' said the future MP. Then he told her he had to go to Paris, or rather to Neuilly to see his old aunt.

'Do you like Paris?' Jessica asked. He said he did. 'It bewilders me, it makes me feel patriotically British, but don't let that stop you from sending me a picture postcard, preferably of the Eiffel Tower.'

'I won't be there long enough.'

Margery was behind the counter. It was four o'clock, and except for two young women seated at a table, yawning with boredom, the bar was empty.

'My darling,' said Margery, and leaned over the bar to kiss him.

'My love,' he said after their long kiss, which the two young women were too bored to notice.

He couldn't tell her about marrying Jessica in front of those two women, and Mme Hermine might make her entry any minute now. He would speak about it when they went to her flat.

'Here's my friend David,' said Mme Hermine, appearing from behind the screen that separated the bar from her office. 'It's lovely to see you two together, a couple of doves. I'm going to make an exception for once. Marge, you can go with David. I won't need you today.'

'Such hard-hearted bawds always have a soft spot for romance,' said Margery as she and David left. 'We're going right to the flat.'

They got straight into bed, and Margery, as though wanting to prove that no woman loved better than she, lifted him to a peak whose existence he hadn't imagined before. He couldn't tell her after such ecstasy that he was marrying, and was therefore about to walk out of her life. At dinner it would be much easier. However, at dinner he couldn't bring it up because they had such a lot to say to each other that he found no room or time to speak of Jessica. Back in the flat it was the same.

He stayed with Margery for three days without broaching the subject. During his return journey to London he decided to leave things as they were. In Jessica's presence he wouldn't think of Margery; in Paris there was no reason to change his relationship with Margery. Anyhow, it was unlikely that in the world she moved in she would ever hear of his marriage.

'You never sent me that postcard,' said Jessica after their first long embrace.

'Because I was thinking all the time of you,' said David.

'I missed you,' said Jessica.

David called over the waiter, paid for his drinks, and took the first street that led to the rue d'Antibes.

There, he thought, was where the rot had set in. No man has two souls, and even if one were given two, besmirching the one couldn't keep the other clean. His tragedy was that he wasn't made to play a double part. It was no good pretending he had been in love with Jessica. Whatever capacity he had for love belonged exclusively to Margery. Jessica had been the fruit of his calculation, whereas Margery had been the lightning that smote him. He had played the double role, and the irony of fate was that he came a cropper though he had acted perfectly. Admittedly it hadn't been too difficult, because the two women were utterly different. One catered for his senses, the other for his ambition. Nowadays his senses were left to their own devices, and ambition had been dead for nearly two decades.

Sylvie let him in.

'Your back hurts?'

'More than ever.'

'Poor Sylvie,' he said, and received a smile that confirmed his suspicion of her having been a streetwalker before the going became too heavy.

Margery lay on the sofa, reading. She looked up, gave him a nod, then returned to the book. 'Help yourself to a drink. I want to finish the chapter.'

2

They sat side by side in the car, Modeste driving, Claud's hand on her knee. If this isn't happiness, he thought, I'll never find out what happiness is.

'Tell me about your father,' said Modeste.

'He was a wonderful man, full of kindness and understanding, and he'd a very high sense of honour. He used to
say when I was small that a mean trick or a nasty thought is
an offence to God, and He isn't angry, only sad.'

'He must have been a wonderful man. Are you Catholics?'

'He was and I am.'

'Your mother?'

'She isn't, but I must say for her that she never sneered or
mocked us.'

'She couldn't have seen you often. She's always in Cannes.'

'She came over once a year. I was brought up by my father
and Lil our housekeeper. Lil is grand, one of the finest persons
I know.'

He went on stroking her knee, now and then she flashed
him a smile. On reaching Villeneuve-Loubet she pulled up in
front of the same house and asked him to wait. Again she
took the baby from the fat woman and walked round the
little garden with it.

'Now we must go back,' she sighed, returning to the car.

'Modeste, I want to kiss you.'

'I want to kiss you, too, but I can't be late. You've no idea
how unpleasant my aunt can become if I'm even a few
minutes late.'

'Will I never kiss you again?'

'You will kiss me, Claud. I want to be kissed by you. I
want it badly. Listen.' She dropped her voice as if afraid her
aunt could overhear her. 'I'll come to your room tonight for
a few minutes, but we must be terribly careful. If she found
out life wouldn't be worth living for me. I don't dare to come
before midnight. Will you be back in the hotel by then?'

'I'll be back much earlier.'

After they had parted at the street corner near the hotel
he sauntered to Alice's London Bar. 'Madame wants you to
go upstairs to the flat,' said Alfred.

Claud found Margery alone in the drawing room. She lay
on the sofa, and he said to himself that his mother either lay
on the sofa or stood downstairs behind the bar. 'Here I am,
mother.'

'Sit down, Claud. Do you want anything to drink?'

'Not really, thank you.'

'I received a short letter from your friend Ludmilla.'

I don't like this, thought Claud. 'What does she say?'

'You can read it. It's on the table.'

'Dear Mrs Darnell,' wrote Ludmilla, 'I hope you are fine, and Claud is enjoying himself. I wish you would tell him not to be lazy and write me the long letter I am expecting from him. I often walk across his land, and I don't think Ringham is making too much of an effort. I feel it is high time for Claud to return. You see my point. Ever yours, Ludmilla Coke.'

'What do you make of it?' asked Margery.

'I'm sure she exaggerates,' said Claud, thinking of Modeste from whom he would be far away if he went back. 'Ringham knows his job, otherwise father wouldn't have kept him. Besides, Ludmilla knows absolutely nothing about farming.'

'You don't speak of her with much affection.'

'It isn't that, but I know Ringham well enough to be certain that she simply invented it.'

'You still want to marry her?'

'What do you think about her, mother?'

'You want my true opinion?'

'Yes, please.'

'If I were a man I wouldn't touch her with a barge pole.'

'Father thought she'd make a very good wife.'

'Do you want a very good wife or a woman who can make you happy?' Claud laughed. 'Don't laugh, I'm serious.'

'A woman who can make me happy,' said Claud, conjuring up Modeste.

'Then wait till you find her. I'd a long chat with Ludmilla's mother after the funeral. They aren't in a hurry, so don't you be in a hurry either. I'm going down to the bar. When you write to her send her my regards.'

Elfrida greeted Claud effusively. She had noticed that David liked him, and she wanted to like anybody David befriended. Also, she was in an excellent mood because of the huge row she'd had with her sister, a successful one in that

Violet had gone off in a huff to Mentone, swearing she wouldn't come near Elfrida again.

'What are you doing tonight?' Elfrida asked Claud.

'Nothing special, but I want to go to bed early.' On no account would he miss Modeste. Fancy her opening his door and not finding him in.

'That suits me,' said Elfrida. 'You'll dine with me, an early dinner, and then you can go straight to bed.'

Claud thanked her, David appeared, she told him she was taking Claud out to dinner, and would David join them.

'Not in a dining mood, thanks all the same.'

The dinner in a far from smart restaurant wasn't any fun for Elfrida. Without David she considered it a flop, and however hard she tried to make conversation she thought she was being dull since her heart wasn't in it. They both sighed their relief when they took leave of one another outside the restaurant. She rushed to Alice's London Bar, he to the Hôtel Romei.

The long wait began, for it was only ten. He had nothing to read which made the time drag. How should he receive Modeste? Should she sit on the bed or in the armchair? The armchair. He would tell her to sit in it, then he would pull up a chair, a feint really, for once she was seated he would bend over her and kiss her as he hadn't kissed before. Would she let him touch her breasts? She had on their outing.

At a few seconds past midnight there was a light rap on the door. He threw it open, and Modeste entered on tiptoe. 'Lock it quickly,' she whispered. He locked the door, turned round, and said, 'Sit in the armchair.'

'I want a kiss first,' she said, meeting him half-way between armchair and door.

They kissed for a while, then she sat down on the bed, he beside her, and as he touched her she unbuttoned the tunic she was wearing. She had no bra, and when he saw the two small round breasts he understood why she didn't have to wear one. 'Kiss them,' she said.

Ecstasy was hardly the word for it. The world had ceased to exist, and the beauty of it was that it had all happened naturally. When she began to undress he undressed, too, as though it had been arranged before. The dark shadow of her pubic hairs, the flat little belly, and above them all the light in her eyes made it so easy that he couldn't help thinking that he had been expecting it from the moment he met her. He saw no reason why it shouldn't continue like that till the end of their lives. With the girl smelling of beer he had felt a little shame and plenty of nausea, but this was so different that he couldn't think of it as a similar act.

'You're the second man in my life,' she said, 'the second and the last. After you I won't look at any other man.'

'You're the first real girl in my life,' said Claud, sitting up the better to gaze at her.

'I love you,' she said, stroking him.

'It's more than love with me. I can't put it into words.'

'Anyway, your French is much more fluent,' she laughed happily.

'Do you speak any English?'

'To the hotel guests, but not to you.'

'Why?'

'I'd be ashamed because it's so bad.'

'You never have to be ashamed of anything, Modeste . . . What's wrong?'

'Nothing,' she said, trying to smile.

After they had made love for the second time she said it was safer for her to go. What would happen if suddenly her aunt went to her room? She and Claud couldn't see each other again.

'I'll come tomorrow night,' she said, throwing her arms round him. 'It was sheer joy.'

She kissed him hard, stood for a few seconds looking at him as if she were taking him in for the first time, and then, before leaving the room, waved as one waves at a railway station. For a while Claud remained in the same position, his eyes on the door, his mind full of her. When he moved at last he half expected to find Modeste in the bed.

He took his trousers off the chair to hang them up. Hearing a rustling sound, he put his hand into the pocket and pulled out Ludmilla's letter to his mother. Ludmilla. He had forgotten her completely, and even thinking of her couldn't bring her back. He had gone swimming with Ludmilla, and thus had a pretty good idea of what her body was like. Modeste's had a golden texture, Ludmilla's was white and pink. Ludmilla laughed a lot because she believed it suited her personality; when Modeste laughed it was to express her joy. He went on finding faults with Ludmilla till he admitted that Ludmilla had become a nuisance because he was in love with Modeste. Before he fell asleep he said to himself that his father would also have preferred Modeste had he known her, which meant he could love Modeste and forget Ludmilla with his father's approval.

The first thing he noticed next morning was Ludmilla's letter. What could he say to her?

On his way to breakfast he saw Modeste facing Mme Romei, who sat behind the large desk, listening humbly to her aunt whose countenance showed that she was upbraiding her niece. Claud stopped to ask whether there was any mail for him, just an excuse to approach Modeste.

'Absolutely nothing for you, monsieur,' said Mme Romei.

Claud looked back from the door : the aunt was at it again. He wished he were a knight of old bursting into the hotel on his palfrey to lift Modeste into the saddle and ride off to his castle with her. He would order his men to raise the draw-bridge if they saw Mme Romei approaching. Entering the writing-room (Rudge had left already) it struck him that with the house, the farm and the money his father had left him he was as much his own master as any knight of old. Modeste flitted through the room. He gave her a protective smile. But what to do about Ludmilla's letter?

After breakfast he went to the café he had been to with David the previous day. He asked for a glass of beer, then took from his pocket a crumpled sheet of paper, which had been there since his arrival in Cannes, and wrote, 'My dear Ludmilla'. So far so good, but what next? He raised his head and looked straight into the hard blue eyes of a Scandinavian girl who sat at the nearest table, a glass of beer in front of her, too. There could be no misunderstanding about the message her eyes conveyed. Claud began to write fast, his eyes glued to the paper.

'Mother showed me your letter. I don't believe for a moment that Ringham isn't doing his best, but even if he didn't I see no reason to rush back.

'I can't say I am having a hectic time, yet I find Cannes enjoyable, and so different from my normal routine. Of course, that doesn't mean that I forget the house and the farm, and I'm sure that after this pleasant rest I'll get down to farming with renewed enthusiasm.'

Claud liked renewed. What more should he say? He couldn't bring himself to send her his love, for his love belonged to Modeste, and he raised his head to look at the Hôtel Romei on the other side of the street. Again he met the Scandinavian girl's hard blue eyes. He lowered his head and wrote, ' "All the best, Miss Ludmilla," as Ron your gardener says. Claud.' Pleased with himself he dashed to the counter to pay for his beer. As he came out of the café he saw Modeste standing in the doorway of the hotel, talking to a hotel guest, waiting for a taxi. My love, he said under his breath, and went to post the letter.

3

Walter woke up in a hideous mood. He had immediately seen a doctor on coming back from Lil. The doctor had attended to hand and leg, yet the hand continued to annoy Walter. Beside him lay Nicole, his wife, snoring her head off. She was on her back, and her open mouth showed her yellow teeth, one of them nearly black. He could strangle her for refusing to go to the dentist. She feared physical pain more than a medieval hermit the Devil. The pouches under her eyes filled him with disgust. 'You old French whore,' he muttered, hoping that would wake her. Nicole snored on.

And this is the woman I married, he said to himself. How could he ever have done that?

Nicole had come over to England, sent by Margery to Miss Hulbert. Walter found her an English husband at the usual rate of one hundred pounds. He couldn't remember the man. Anyhow, they were all the same sort. The husband and Nicole parted outside the registry office, and Nicole settled down in London to earn money for Miss Hulbert, Victor and Margery. However, one day the husband turned up again, wanting a divorce because he had found some woman who had a small shop and was ready to marry him. Usually the husbands vanished for ever, and, if they married bigamously, that was none of Walter's business. But Nicole's husband was a pain in the neck, and afraid lest he cause trouble a divorce was arranged and paid for. During these transactions Walter saw more of Nicole than was good for his peace of mind. Not only did he go to bed with her several times, but he got so accustomed to her that he married her in the end. Miss Hulbert said she saw no reason why Nicole shouldn't continue her call-girl career. Remembering that he considered himself a gentleman, Walter refused to let her work. Victor approved. 'Business is one thing,' said Victor, 'private life is another. Take Lil. In no circumstances would I have allowed her to go with men after she became my housekeeper. With a wife it's even more essential.'

It was fine and splendid to have that excellent performer in bed at his beck and call, but after ten years it had worn thin. She was the sort that aged quickly, was lazy and untidy, lacked brains yet had all the cunning of a Norman peasant.

'I'm getting up,' said Walter.

Nicole opened her blue eyes, looked at him as if she weren't quite sure who he was, then turned on her side. She had grown fat, had no waist left, and every night Walter complained of her taking up all the room in the bed. He went to the window which, despite the warm weather, was kept closed because Nicole feared fresh air. He opened it to annoy her, looked out, decided for the hundredth time that he loathed Shaftesbury Avenue, then he went to the bathroom. Dirty underclothes were soaking in the bath. He swore loudly before he took the lot out, throwing them on a chair. He shaved while he ran his bath. Something was wrong with the taps, the water trickled slowly, taking ages to fill the bath. Every day he repeated to Nicole that she should telephone the plumber. Trust Nicole not to.

Standing in front of the shaving glass, that hadn't been cleaned since yesterday's shave, he thought for no special reason of the late Victor. That man, he said to himself, could wallow in dirt without it leaving any trace on him. He had thrown himself into the white slave traffic after he married Margery, and when he had made his packet he pulled out with the airs of a nobleman who has got tired of the jeu de paume. Why, Walter suddenly wondered, hadn't Victor wanted Lil to know that he, Walter, had married Nicole whom Lil had surely met while working for Miss Hulbert? Was it not to give Lil ideas above her station? Walter shook his head. Victor didn't want Lil to know about it because he considered it sordid to marry a prostitute, he who had lived on the money they earned. Anger shook Walter and he cut his chin, which didn't improve his temper.

Victor had considered himself a superior being, a man of honour, too, and looked down on Walter for being married to Nicole. True, he never said so, yet his behaviour showed it. What right had Victor to look down on Nicole? Was it because he had married Margery late from Pigalle, whom he, Walter, had laid for the meagre sum of a thousand old francs? Margery had been twice the whore that Nicole was, for she had been decently brought up whereas poor Nicole was a poor bastard from Elbeuf who'd had to make her way all on her own. And why had lofty Victor married Margery? Walter laughed, for that was truly a good one.

He got into the bath. The water wasn't hot enough, so he didn't bother to wash, and when he climbed out his temper was even worse. Nicole was sitting up in bed, her face greasy, her double chin in evidence. Her torn night dress showed her hanging breasts.

'Gosh, you look ugly,' said Walter.

'What about you with that huge belly and yellow legs? No

woman in her right mind would ever touch you, the disgusting sight that you are.'

'That's where you're wrong, you old cow,' said Walter, and as he spoke Lil appeared in front of him, and he saw himself throwing her on the sofa, lying on top of her, and she fighting like a wild cat. He felt such hatred that he could have strangled Nicole because he couldn't lay his hands on Lil.

'Show me one,' said Nicole, 'but you can't, you fat, old, ugly pig.'

'That's enough,' said Walter, and had a good mind to box her ears. It wouldn't be the first time. However, a notion came to him that brought a new light to his eyes.

Lil didn't want him because he was apparently a fat, old, ugly pig. To give him two thousand pounds to keep his trap closed was one thing, to open her legs for him wasn't part of the bargain. He would repay Lil in her own coin. She trusted his honour yet wouldn't take his cock. She would regret it till her dying day. What a perfect revenge, not only on her but on Victor, too. My son, my boy, but Victor had overlooked the fact that he had been paid to be able to say 'My son, my boy'. How condescending Victor had been to him when he came out of the cooler. 'You shouldn't have embezzled, Walter, but I promise not to bring it up again.' That was a good one, too. Mr David Woodlow had sent him a fiver; not a word with it. David would pay also. He would be working on an enormous canvas, Lil in despair, Margery furious, the boy turning on Victor, hating his memory, and David forced to admit he was the father, for which the boy would hate him, too.

'I'm going to France in a day or two, Nicole,' he said in a friendly voice.

'Go to France or to hell, I don't care,' said Nicole.

Walter wasn't the only person thinking of visiting Claud on the Riviera. Mr Coke who had just arrived for a few days' stay with wife and daughter, was at that very hour advising Ludmilla to fly out to Claud.

Father, mother and daughter were breakfasting when Gretchen brought in Claud's letter. Ludmilla tore the envelope open, read the letter twice before she said to Mrs Coke, 'I don't like it. Read it, mother.'

'I don't like it either,' said Mrs Coke.

'You don't like what?' asked Mr Coke, who bore a striking resemblance to his daughter.

'Read it,' said Mrs Coke. 'It's from Claud Darnell whom Ludmilla intends to marry.'

'I don't intend. I'm going to,' said Ludmilla.

'I remember him,' said Mr Coke, 'a very nice chap.'

'Doesn't sound so nice in his letter,' said Ludmilla.

Mr Coke read it, then said, 'I don't think Romeo would have written such a letter to Juliet.'

'Romeo and Juliet, that's a lot of hooey,' said Ludmilla. 'I'd never let him climb into my room, and I wouldn't die for him. Ours is a far healthier relationship.'

'In that case,' said her father, 'there's nothing to worry about.'

'Anyway, he'll be back soon,' said Mrs Coke, itching to go out to the garden.

'And if he isn't,' said Ludmilla who had expected that her letter to Margery would bring Claud flying back.

'There are no ifs in life,' said Mrs Coke. She smiled at them, then went out through the french window.

'Are you very fond of him?' asked Mr Coke.

'I want to marry him. Mind you, there's no great hurry, but nothing will stop me from marrying him.'

'Is he as keen on it as you?'

'Of course.'

'It isn't "of course", Ludmilla. Your being keen on marrying him is no proof of his being equally keen on it. He's younger than you, isn't he?'

'He is, but that doesn't count.'

'It counts insofar as he is perhaps still too young to be as decided as you. Males reach maturity much later than females.'

'Don't frighten me, papa,' said Ludmilla.

'I don't want to frighten you, I only want you to look at it dispassionately. You say you're in no hurry. When do you intend to marry him?'

'In a year or two.'

'You speak as though it mattered little to you, my child.'

'It matters a lot, but I'm happy here, so I don't see any reason to precipitate matters.'

Mr Coke looked at his daughter, who returned his gaze, and then said, shaking his head, 'If I were you I wouldn't go on with it. You're not in love with him.'

'I am.'

'If you were you'd be in a hurry to marry him. May I ask you a question?'

'Of course, papa.'

'Is Claud your lover?'

'In what sense?' Ludmilla asked, thinking of their hugging and kissing, nothing wrong in that.

'In the only sense.'

'You mean going to bed with him?'

'Exactly.'

'I don't go to bed with him. I don't believe in going to bed with the man one wants to marry.'

'Admirable logic,' smiled Mr Coke, 'and it proves perfectly that you don't really care for him. Chuck it, Ludmilla.'

Ludmilla thought that over. She couldn't picture herself going to bed with Claud; she couldn't see herself lying down with him at night and waking up with him in the morning; for morning meant opening her eyes in her bedroom, smiling at the sky-blue curtains and striped wallpaper; night meant reading in bed, then lying on her belly to await sleep. 'Perhaps,' she said half aloud. She gasped, as plain, ugly jealousy gripped her. It was out of the question to allow some other woman to take over her little brother.

'I won't chuck it,' she said, flushing. 'I'm going to marry him. If necessary I'll marry him straight away.'

'In that case fly out to Cannes and bring him back.'

'What did you say?'

'You heard me. If you really want him don't dither. Go out.'

'What will mummy say?'

'You're not marrying your mother, my child.'

'You do say funny things at times, papa,' Ludmilla laughed.
'I'm not trying to be funny. I'm dead serious.'
'Don't look so solemn. I promise I'll think it over.'
'Don't think it over in your mother's company.'

4

When David arrived to lunch with Margery he found her alone in the dark drawing room.

'Where's Claud?' he asked.

'He rang up to say he was going to Grasse for the day. Why? Do you miss your son?'

'Don't say that even as a joke.'

'We both know he is, and, as I've said before, blood is thicker than water.'

'And I'll answer again that you make me laugh. Let's talk of something else.'

'I never have to search for subjects,' said Margery. 'I didn't want to tell you last night in front of Elfrida because she's such a chatterbox.'

'What is it?'

'Mrs Gillies, the German lesbian, declared her passion for me yesterday afternoon. She said she'd fallen in love with me.'

'What did you answer?' asked David in an uneasy voice. He had become accustomed long ago to her having lovers, and he had no right or reason to complain. However, this was new, and in their relationship he wanted nothing new and nothing strange.

'I told her not to be silly, and, since she persisted, I said I didn't want to give her and her husband a new kick. She became purple with anger, and last night they didn't turn up in the bar. That won't ruin me.'

'Le déjeuner est servi,' sighed Sylvie from the door.

During the meal David and Margery had little to say to one another. Now and then he glanced at her, she wasn't looking in his direction. However, when Sylvie had brought in the coffee their eyes suddenly met. He quickly turned away, for their expression reminded him of a painful Saturday afternoon in Paris about which neither of them liked to think, he even less than she.

Jessica's uncle had found David a constituency in his native Norfolk. The Labour MP was killed in a motor accident, his majority had been two thousand, and it looked pretty probable that the new Labour candidate, no older than David, would keep the constituency for his party. The uncle and the local Conservative agent had no illusions about David's chances of winning the seat for the Conservatives, but, as the uncle pointed out, if he put up a good show an easier constituency would be found for him before the General Elections. David rushed into the fray, full of enthusiasm. He and Jessica married immediately, since it is a considerable help if a candidate has an attractive wife. Between them they possessed enough dogs to give their photograph, distributed to the electors, the true blue Tory touch.

They went for a brief honeymoon in Scotland, then settled down to electioneering. Jessica was a frigid woman who deeply resented her frigidity. David took to heart the old adage of there being no frigid women, only clumsy men. Jessica tried her hardest, yet the result was mutual dissatisfaction which they hid from each other since they were both determined to make a success of their marriage. The electorate want their MPs happily married. In order to show that he could take it in his stride, David made love nearly every night to Jessica, whose peace of mind was restored only on the nights when he didn't. In the daytime they were the ideal couple, and all who met them were moved by their team work in trying to defeat his opponent in the field.

One Friday afternoon he told Jessica that he wished to spend the weekend in Paris, as he wanted to look up his old aunt in Neuilly who was a bedridden invalid. Jessica said she would come, too. He did his best to dissuade her, saying the old woman liked no new faces, that her doctors forbade her any sort of excitement, he, the nephew, hadn't even written to tell her that he had got married.

'Doesn't she read newspapers?' Jessica asked.

'She reads nothing because of her very bad eyesight. You told me, darling, that you don't care for Paris. You'd be bored stiff if you came. You can do so much for me while I'm away.'

Jessica wanted to do all she could for him to compensate him for the fiasco in bed. So she remained. He flew over on Saturday morning and went straight to the rue des Capucines. Margery herself opened the door to him.

'At last, my love,' she cried, embracing him. 'I was waiting and waiting.'

Those words proved that she hadn't read any English newspapers, hence didn't know that he was married.

'I couldn't come before,' he said, his eyes shining as he took in the one woman he truly loved.

She was wearing a dressing gown, and with his arms round her he could feel the warmth of her body. Jessica's seemed invariably cold. He pushed her straight into the bedroom, where they fell on the unmade bed.

Lifting his eyes from the coffee cup, David looked at Margery who was watching two flies approaching the sugar basin. You gave me more than I hoped for or expected, yet it did me for life. He wouldn't have been surprised if she had heard those unuttered words. Margery continued observing the flies.

He and Margery made love as if to make up for all the time they had lost, which included his nights with his wife. Margery rose to answer the door bell, and he remained on the bed, contented and happy.

'It was the concierge,' she said, coming back. 'A letter for the woman who owns this flat. I must send it on to her.' She sat down on the bed, and put her hands on his naked chest. 'My adored David, I've got some extraordinary news for you. I'm pregnant.'

The sun dropped out of the sky, the night came at once, hurling down the stars and the moon. The result was that David lost his head. He didn't regain it for a considerable time. He was married to Jessica, in a few weeks he might be an MP with a great career in front of him, but all that was shattered by the woman whose hands were on his chest.

'Impossible,' he cried, jumping up. 'Impossible.'

'The doctor told me it's certain. I'll be the mother of your child, my love. David, isn't it wonderful?'

'It's the worst thing that could have happened to me,' he shouted, ready to strangle her or collapse on the floor, never to rise again.

'Don't look at me like that. You frighten me, David. It's no tragedy.'

'It's the worst tragedy, a deadly tragedy, it's my ruin.'

'Because I carry your child? You're hiding something from me.'

'I got married three weeks ago, Margery. Your child will be my undoing.'

'It's not true. How could you get married? We love each other completely.'

'It's my career, it's my future,' he mumbled.

'Going already?' asked Margery as he rose from the table. 'You look flushed. What's wrong, David?'

'I need fresh air,' said David, starting for the door. 'Sylvie's cuisine du Nord is far too heavy for this weather. See you later.'

It wasn't fresh air he needed, he admitted as he flew down the stairs. It was his shame he wanted to take out of her flat for fear she might smell it. For the shame of it was that in his fear of losing the shining political career he had mapped out for himself he had ceased to trust Margery, whom he should have trusted more than anyone he had ever met.

He sat down on a café terrace next to a small group of young German tourists who were laughing a lot while shouting at each other at the top of their voices. He asked for a large brandy, swallowing it in one gulp a second after the waiter had put the glass and the saucer on the table.

While Margery was staring at him, her mouth open, tears gathering in her eyes, his thoughts were of the meanest kind. The woman late of Pigalle, the assistant procuress of fat Mme Hermine, now held the whip. She could go to Jessica and tell her she was carrying Jessica's husband's child, that David was her lover, simply adored her, came to Paris to find his true happiness in her arms. Jessica was a woman of principles, her every word betrayed that. She would consider herself cheated and besmirched, and would walk out on him without listening to his entreaties, rightly so since he had lied to her from the very beginning. With Jessica gone, his career would be shattered, no future left for him. Trust her uncle to make sure of that. He was in the presence of this erstwhile prostitute, that is to say he was in her power, in short his fate depended on her.

'Your career, your future,' he heard her repeating his words. 'For God's sake, David, what do careers and futures matter when two people love each other as we love each other.'

'I'm married, and you're going to have a child.'

'You married to make a career. I don't mind, honestly I don't, as long as you go on loving me.'

Cunning creature, he thought, so this is the game you're going to play? He saw himself never having a moment's peace of mind, the sword of Damocles a toothpick compared with the power she could wield. The junior minister trembling whenever the telephone rang; the member of the cabinet fearing his own shadow because the cunning creature might see it. What was she saying?'

'David, don't look so crestfallen. I won't have an abortion. You can't have one in France and besides, I want to keep it in memory of you. But how could you have got married, David? You're rich, you don't need a career, and I love you as no woman has ever loved a man. Look at yourself, you don't even dare to look at me. You went from my arms to marry some bloody woman because she has the right connections. Isn't it so?'

He didn't answer, his eyes were glued to the carpet which had two large holes. What was the blackmailer saying?

'Of course it's so, but you wanted le chou et la chèvre, my great David. If I hadn't told you I was pregnant you'd have gone on pretending you weren't married.'

'I expect to be elected MP in a couple of weeks' time.'

'A pity I don't live in that constituency.'

'Why is it a pity?' he asked. The blackmail was beginning.

'If I lived there I'd vote for you,' she said, laughing hysterically.

'Stop it,' he shouted.

'I can't,' she said, continuing to laugh.

He started to dress, turning his back on her. Suddenly, he felt her hands on his shoulders. 'What do you want?' he asked gruffly.

'Nothing, David, and for God's sake don't get panicky. I won't be the first or the last unmarried mother. In my world a married mother is a freak of nature. All I want from you is that you come over now and then to see your whore of yore.' She laughed. 'Whore of yore. I like that.'

She was deep, but not deep enough for him. If he were to continue seeing her he would remain under her thumb, having to obey her whims and caprices. If not, she would go to Jessica and that would be his end. She could do that now, in six months' time, in a year, in ten years. Never would he find peace again.

'Answer me, my poor frightened darling,' she said. He remained silent because he was thinking hard, searching for a way out. 'I bet your wife looks like nothing on earth.'

'She's beautiful and she's a great lady.'

'Which I am not and never want to be. I mean a great lady. You must have guessed that. Now stop looking so green and panicky. I won't interfere with your great career. I make enough money to bring up the child, so stop worrying, and smile. I'm going to have my bath. Come and keep me company.'

He shook his head. She laughed to herself as she went to the bathroom. He sat down on the bed, as exhausted as if he had charged enemy troops in thick mud. When she said she wouldn't interfere with his career she proved finally that she couldn't be trusted. She would go on saying that as long as it suited her, but sooner or later she would discover that his marriage with Jessica worked perfectly, that it wasn't only a matter of helping him in his career. Then she would strike. A woman who could earn her living on her back and who wasn't ashamed of being a procuress was capable of any mean trick. He heard her getting out of the bath. As she opened the door the solution came to him. He felt like going on his knees to thank God for saving him.

'We can arrange everything, my love,' he said.

'We don't have to arrange anything, David. I'll have the child, bring it up myself, and you go on concentrating on your career.'

I'm cleverer than you, he said to himself. Then aloud, 'The child must have a father.'

'He has one.'

'I mean an official father. I don't want it to be illegitimate. Also you must have a proper home to bring the child up in. I think, in fact I'm almost certain, that I've got the father. The home will be provided by me. Within a few days I'll arrange the whole business.'

'Don't talk so mysteriously,' said Margery, sitting down beside him on the bed, her body smelling of bath salts. He wanted her again, and throwing his arms round her warm body it struck him that making love to her could simplify matters a lot. True, he forgot everything once he had penetrated her. None-the-less he blushed, looking at the empty glass of brandy in front of him. The German tourists were still laughing and shouting.

'We'll never be able to leave each other,' Margery said happily when they rose from the bed, and he had to start dressing again.

'We never will,' he said, proud of himself being the cunning one this time. 'Listen to me carefully, my darling. Do you remember Victor Darnell?'

'The friend of yours who said he never paid a woman and whom we saw at the Deux Magots?'

'That's the one.'

'What about him?'

'I want you to marry him, thus the child will have an official father.'

'Aren't you a wee bit off your head, my darling? Why should he want to marry me?'

He told her about taking Victor to his house near Dover,

of Victor's reaction to the house, his asking him to give him the house, as you ask for a match, and his repeating his mad demand while she was telephoning at the Deux Magots. 'I'll give him the house if he marries you, treats the child as his own, in short behaves as a husband and a father should.'

'As long as I don't have to go to bed with him. I want only you.'

'My wonderful darling,' he said, beaming on her. 'Anyway, you won't have to worry about that. The house is all that matters to him.'

His plan was faultless. The house near Dover he hadn't mentioned to Jessica yet, so he could give it away without her being any the wiser. Besides it wouldn't be giving it away, for Victor would buy it with money that David would give him. Thus none would know the real state of affairs. Once Margery was married to Victor she couldn't do him any mischief. Going to Jessica, declaring that her child wasn't her husband's but David's would sound like a cock and bull story, and he had enough influence over his wife to persuade her that poor Mrs Darnell was stark raving mad. Besides, Margery was intelligent enough to know that she couldn't get away with it.

'Do you believe for a moment that I'm going to live buried in the English countryside?' asked Margery.

'Once you're married and the child is installed in the house, which, if I remember rightly, is called the White House probably because the walls are yellow, you'll do whatever you want. Anyway, you never do anything you don't want to. If Victor dies first, the house will be left to you and the child. I'll see to that. Thus you'll both be provided for.'

Margery looked at him as if wanting to study him from a new angle. David turned his head away, saying, 'The perfect solution.' He couldn't return her gaze because he had the uneasy feeling that she understood his motives. 'The perfect solution,' he repeated. 'Now we can go out to lunch.'

'Perhaps it won't be a bad thing to have an official husband, especially an English one.'

'What do you mean?'

134

'I can't tell it to a future MP, my darling. Anyway, it only concerns me.'

'I see,' he said, thinking that the less he knew the better it would be for him in the long run.

He took her to a restaurant in the Halles, and in his immense relief he was the life and soul of their little party. His buoyancy regained, he hardly noticed Margery's long silences. In the afternoon she went to Mme Hermine, he fetched her towards midnight, and he seldom had enjoyed a night more than the one that followed. Next day he flew back to London, took a taxi to his flat, and telephoned Victor. The number didn't answer. Supposing Victor had disappeared or gone to jail as Walter had? He was in despair. He tried the number several times, no luck. He dined in his club, dialled the number on his return, and he nearly cried out with joy as he heard Victor's voice.

'David Woodlow speaking. Can you come round to my flat, Victor? I've got some really marvellous news for you.'

'Is it about your house near Dover?'

He does have a one-track mind, David couldn't help saying to himself. 'It is about the house.'

'I'm coming round at once.'

'Good. I'll put a bottle of champagne into the bucket. We'll celebrate.'

Though Victor lived in digs at the other end of London he managed to turn up surprisingly quickly, looking as dignified as ever in his threadbare suit, not a husband to be ashamed of.

'Victor,' said David pouring out champagne, 'you can have the house, but I warn you there's a condition attached to it.'

'I accept it even before I hear about it,' said Victor with shining eyes. 'Even if it means murdering somebody.'

'Nothing as elaborate,' laughed David. 'Do you remember Margery?'

'Who's she?'

'The tall English girl we met in Pigalle shortly before we were demobbed.'

'The one who went with you and Walter?'

'That's the one,' said David, wishing he could box Victor's ears, which was of course out of the question. 'You can have the house as a gift if you marry her. She's pregnant, and I want her child to be legitimate. I have my reasons for it.'

'I won't ask what they are,' said Victor grandly.

'Anyway, I leave you to guess them as long as you keep your trap closed. That's part of our bargain too.'

'I quite understand that.'

'Have more champagne, Victor. So you marry Margery, when the child is born you'll treat it as your own, and go on doing so till it grows up. If you die you leave the house to Margery and your child.'

'Quite,' said Victor.

'So we're all happy now,' said David, lifting his glass. 'I got married the other day.'

'Saw it in *The Times*. Congratulations.'

'Thank you, my dear Victor. How's Walter getting on since his release?'

'Not too well. He has an almost menial job.'

'He should have been more circumspect.'

'It's easy for you to talk, but I agree with you. Embezzling isn't gentlemanly. Still, the poor fellow paid for it. Naturally, the farm goes with the house.'

'What?' said David, jumping up. 'I never thought of the farm. It's rather a large farm, worth a lot of money.'

'You can't expect a person like me who earns only a few pounds a week in a house agent's office to be able to keep up a house like that. There must be an income with it. Besides I've always wanted to farm.'

'I see your point,' said David. The last thing he wanted was for Victor to back out now. 'Mind you, the farm is let for another five years.'

'I'll survive till then,' said Victor.

'I can help you a bit.'

'If you want the wife and the child to live in the house you'll have to help a little.'

'I most certainly want them to live there. We'll discuss that when she comes over.'

Victor left only at two in the morning. Before going, he said, 'David, Walter lives in utter misery. I know it's his own fault, I'm the last person to approve of dishonesty, but he's my protégé in a way.'

David looked away so that Victor shouldn't see the merriment in his eyes, for nothing could be funnier than Victor having a protégé. He gave Victor a cheque for twenty pounds made out to Walter. 'Remember he's not under my wing. I won't give him any more.'

'I appreciate that,' said Victor.

David rang up Margery after the front door had closed on Victor. He asked her to come over as soon as she could. 'I'm not in a hurry,' she said.

'We must fix it as soon as possible.'

'All right, I'll be in London on Thursday. Is that soon enough for you?'

She's trying to sound sarcastic, he thought after he had thanked her.

She married Victor ten days later, and David was elected MP a fortnight afterwards with a majority of twelve hundred. He was wildly cheered by the Opposition as he made his entry in the House. Fair stood the wind for a fine career.

David paid for the double brandy, left the café terrace, and as he turned the corner his mind went back to a visit to Paris soon after the election, his intention being to see the newly wed Mrs Darnell, who wasn't taking up residence in White House till her pregnancy was more advanced, and to spend the night with her. She was behind the counter in Mme Hermine's bar. The time was nearly midnight. She gave him her customary smile, he chatted with Mme Hermine, and when Margery was ready to leave they went out together. He talked about his maiden speech which he would be making in a few weeks. She listened, continuing to smile. On reaching the porte cochère of the house in the rue des Capucines he lifted his finger to press the button to open the door. She pulled his hand down.

'You're not coming in,' she said in a quiet voice. 'I'll never go to bed with you as long as I live. You didn't trust me, you didn't believe in me, you miserable little Machiavelli. Get out of my life once and for all.'

He stood staring at her, and couldn't think of anything to say because what she said was true. She pressed the button, the door flew open, and stepping across the threshold she called over her shoulder, 'You don't have to give any money to Victor. I'll look after him as long as it's needed.'

David heard the German tourists behind him, and stopped to let them go past. He noticed he was standing in front of a florist's window. He ought to send Margery a dozen roses, anonymously of course. But then she might think it was Mrs Gillies who had sent them.

He walked on.

VI

1

Claud came back from Grasse towards evening. Had any one asked him what he saw in Grasse he could truthfully have answered that he saw only Modeste, who had embedded herself in his thoughts, taking up all the room. Once or twice he had tried to remember Ludmilla. It was in vain, for Modeste pushed her away. Whenever he glanced at his watch he added up the hours that still separated him from her. He looked into the hotel, and there she sat behind the small desk, her aunt lording it behind the large one.

'Absolutely no letters for you, monsieur,' said Mme Romei.

'Is Monsieur David in?' he asked Modeste, just an excuse to hear her voice.

'He went out at noon,' said Mme Romei before Modeste could open her mouth.

'Thank you, madame,' said Claud, his and Modeste's eyes met for a second and, refreshed as it were, he strolled to Alice's London Bar.

'Here's Claud,' said Elfrida, waving to him. 'He's such a nice boy, don't you think, David?'

'Hullo, Claud,' said David. 'Come to the bar, I've got something to tell you.'

Disappointed, Elfrida watched them stopping at the bar where David told Alfred to serve them beer.

'You don't have to drink it,' said David. 'I just wanted to get away from her. Do you want to dine with me? Don't answer me too loudly because I don't want her to overhear us.'

'With pleasure,' whispered Claud, which made David laugh. 'But what about mother?'

'She has plenty of people to keep her company.'

David took him to the restaurant where he dined most evenings on noodles.

'Tell me please about my father when he was a soldier,' said Claud after they had had their fill of spaghetti.

'He was a very brave soldier and an excellent leader of men.'

'Were you in action with him?'

'In Normandy, later in Belgium.'

'And you were great friends?'

'Very much so, real comrades in arms.'

'Yet you never came to White House.'

'That's because I live in France.'

'I begin to like France a lot.'

'Tell me, Claud, but don't tell me if you don't want to, is there a French skirt behind your liking for France? Don't blush, dear boy.' Claud nodded. 'May I make another guess? Is she by any chance called Modeste? You're pink, Claud.'

'How did you guess?'

'She's blossomed out since your arrival, and so have you.'

'She's awfully nice.'

'I agree.'

'You've known her for a long time, haven't you?'

'Ever since she came to live with her aunt.'

'So you know her well?'

'Quite well, and I can only praise her.'

As he said that, David remembered Modeste's misadventure with the student. Should he mention it to Claud? It would be truly funny, in a macabre fashion to tell Claud that Modeste had a little bastard. But it would be unfair on them, and on him to.

'I'm so glad you like her,' said Claud.

'What about the girl in England?'

'I don't know because I'm certain now that I care only for Modeste.'

'Then forget her, my boy,' said David, putting his hand on Claud's sleeve. 'If you love then don't dither, don't shilly-shally. Nothing is worse than losing or giving up a person who really matters to you.'

He smiled on Claud, thinking that, had he himself taken the advice he was giving to the young man, he would now be dining with his wife and son, probably in Brinworth Hall. However, you can't change your instincts and aspirations, and he hoped for Claud's sake that his instincts were better than his and that he had no aspirations of the kind that he had had. Jessica appeared before him, dying of leukaemia, smiling to encourage him to hope, brave to the last. He hardly heard Claud, saying 'Thank you so much. I won't forget what you said.'

'But first be sure you're serious.'

'I am.'

'Lucky boy.'

He's one of the nicest men I ever met, said Claud to himself after they had parted outside Alice's London Bar, almost as nice as father was. He sighed because his father couldn't meet Modeste.

He stopped to chat with the night porter in the hope that Modeste would come through the hall. The night porter had eaten shrimps before he came to work, and shrimps didn't agree with him. He enlarged on shrimps and the pain in his stomach, a pain that resembled a railway engine on fire because it went up and down inside him. Claud commiserated with him, then escaped to his room to start the vigil. Supposing she couldn't come? He got on his knees to pray that she would.

She knocked lightly on the door at five to twelve. He flung it open with such ardour that the lamp on the bedside table shook. 'Don't make a noise,' she whispered, though her eyes were aglow with pleasure. She wore a new dress, and her hair showed she had been to the hairdresser. They kissed, then she sat down on the bed, and he beside her. He put his arm round her waist, and for a little while they said nothing as there seemed to be no need to speak, move or think. Footsteps going past the door shattered the silence.

'I can recognise the footsteps,' Modeste whispered. 'M. Rudge, nobody stamps like him.'

'He's dotty.'

'And wicked.'

'That also?'

'If he sees me speaking to any of the male hotel guests he reports it to my aunt.'

'Disgusting man,' said Claud, and leaving the waist his hand touched her left breast.

'Want me to undress?' she asked.

'Nothing I want more.'

She stood up and undressed, with his eyes following her every movement. When she stood naked in front of him, her eyes sparkling under the long eyelashes, he felt more ache than desire, the ache rising in him like the burning railway engine of the night porter.

'I love you, Claud,' she said. 'Let me lie down on the bed.'

That brought him, so to speak, back to his senses. He threw his things off, and her arms and legs opened for him. It was an offering, the best present she could think of. As their bodies moved and shook the ache was back, and to get rid of it he cried out, 'Modeste, I want to marry you.' Her eyes said she heard him, her body answered for her. When they had reached the climax she burst into tears.

'What is it, Modeste?' he asked as their bodies separated.

'You should never have said that to me,' she sobbed.

'But I meant it and I mean it. I want you to marry me. I couldn't be happy with any other woman.'

'You say that so beautifully, mon vrai chéri, but it's impossible. Nobody regrets it more than I.'

'It is possible, nothing and nobody can stop us.' Ludmilla ceased being even a memory. 'I'm my own master. My father left everything he had to me.'

'I repeat it's impossible. Give me a handkerchief.'

As he fetched it an awful notion struck him. Was she married? Only marriage could stand between them. 'Are you married?' he asked, holding out a handkerchief. She wiped her eyes before answering, 'I have a child.'

'A child? So you're married, Modeste.'

'I'm not married, yet I have a child. Now you understand?'

She turned on her belly to cry into the pillow. His eyes were on her golden behind while his mind tried to cope with the sudden problem of which he could make neither head nor tail. He touched the behind and stroked it.

'For nobody on earth,' she sobbed into the pillow, 'will I give up my child. It's bad enough to have it in Villeneuve-Loubet, but I won't let it go any farther from me.'

'Is that the baby I saw the other day?'

'You saw it twice.'

'That's right,' he said, but that didn't solve the problem. 'It looked a very sweet baby.'

'You're wonderful, Claud,' she said, turning on her back, her cheeks shining with tears. 'I don't deserve you.'

'I don't see anything catastrophic in your having a child, my Modeste.'

'Don't you understand my child is illegitimate? My aunt calls it the fruit of my sin.'

'Bother your aunt,' said Claud, sitting down on the bed.

'She's right in the eyes of the world. I love you so, I wish as I never wished anything before, that it was your child, but it isn't.' She sat up. 'It isn't.'

'Once we're married and we live in England we can pretend it's our child.'

'You're a saint, Claud,' she said, grabbing his hand and kissing it. Lil, he thought, pulling his hand away, would laugh her head off if she could hear him called a saint. 'Don't you understand that the child had a father, and that I went to bed with him?'

'I'm not that ignorant,' he couldn't help smiling. 'I'm old enough to know that babies don't grow under rose bushes.'

'What a pity,' she sighed. He bent down to kiss her. 'I must tell you everything, my saintly Claud. There was here a young man, Alain Monteclain, a student at the University of Marseilles who, to earn a little extra money during his holidays, acted as night porter over the weekends. He's the father.'

'He's gone I hope.'

'For ever. When I told him I was pregnant he looked pleased. We both spoke to my aunt, telling her we wanted to get married. As I was pregnant I expected her to say yes. I wasn't of age yet. My aunt refused to hear of it, thank God.

She called Alain a fortune hunter, worse than a gigolo, who wanted to marry me only to get hold of her hotel and the two houses she possesses in Nice. But we could marry if we felt like it. She could disinherit me, and never would we see a centime of hers. On that Alain scuttled back to Marseilles, and I never heard from him again.'

'There's no such fear where I'm concerned,' said Claud. 'I don't need or want any of your aunt's money.'

'You really want to go on with it after all I told you?'

'I want to marry you. The child will come with us when we go to England.'

She threw her arms round him, cried out of sheer happiness, and went on repeating that he was a saint and she didn't deserve him. 'I'll dedicate my whole life to you, my saint.'

'Frankly, I don't like being called a saint, Modeste. Makes me feel old.'

He asked her how old the child was. Just over a year. Boy or girl? A girl called Marie-Bénédicte. The best idea was, he said, to say in England that she had been married before, and that her husband had died soon after the wedding. Thus Marie-Bénédicte would be considered his stepdaughter. England was full of married men who had stepdaughters.

'How clever you are,' Modeste said admiringly.

'I'm cunning, mon amour.'

'And you won't change your mind? Can I really count on you?'

'You can always count on my father's son.'

She stayed with him till nearly dawn, and when, regretfully, she rose from the bed he asked her when would they tell her aunt about it.

'Let's wait a day or two,' she said. 'I'm terrified of her.'

'But no longer,' he called after her.

The bed smelt of the scent she used, and he found a hairpin on the pillow which he decided to keep in memory of the night. When he rose in the morning he was even more determined to marry her than when he had proposed to her. The telephone bell rang. Who could it be? Only his mother. 'Yes,' he said.

'It's Lil. I called your mother last night, she gave me your number. I just wanted to know how you were. Are you all right, Claud?'

'I'm fine, Lil. How nice of you to ring me. How are you?'

'Very well, thank you.'

'How's Wilf?'

'He's standing beside me.'

'Pat him in my name.'

'When are you coming back?'

'I don't know yet.'

'Don't hurry, Claud. No need to. You sound very cheerful.'

'As a matter of fact I am.'

'I'm glad. God bless.'

Lil rang off. Good old Lil, he thought, would love Modeste. He remembered her saying she intended to leave. He would persuade her to stay, bringing up Modeste's child as the excuse.

Modeste wasn't around when he came down. 'This being Sunday I'll have my breakfast when I come back from Mass,' he said to the waiter. He took himself to Notre-Dame-de-Bon-Voyage, and the first person he saw on entering the church was Modeste in the last but one row. There was room beside her. The glance he received from her moved him so deeply that he wanted to ask her again to marry him and bring Marie-Bénédicte to England.

'Isn't it marvellous that we went to the same Mass?' she said as they came out.

'It's a matter of instinct,' he laughed.

'Do you still mean all you said in the night? I won't hold you to it.'

'I repeat, I'm my father's son.'

She asked him not to accompany her to the hotel as she didn't want her aunt to see them together. 'I promise I'll overcome my fear in a day or two,' she said. 'Can you come with me to Villeneuve-Loubet this afternoon? I'll pick you up at three o'clock at the corner.'

So he held Marie-Bénédicte in his arms while her mother gazed at him as a believer does at the statue of a saint. He held the child clumsily, and, being still too near to his childhood to see anything moving in a year-old baby, he was pleased when Modeste took her from him. 'A dear little thing,' he said in answer to the look in Modeste's eyes.

2

Margery could wallow for an hour in her bath, smoking one cigarette after the other. Michel had rung up to inform her he was back, that he was glad she was back from England, and when could he see her. She said she would telephone him in his chambers in a day or two. She wasn't yet awake enough to tell him that she wasn't keen on seeing him again.

After her second cigarette she thought of Claud, whom she found to be a more amusing person in Cannes than she had in the White House during her short visits (which she had invariably considered a bore while Victor lived). After his death he had ceased to be even a shadow. When she and he came out of the registry office in the company of their two witnesses, Walter and some woman whose name she had forgotten long ago, she declared she was flying back to Paris in the afternoon.

'You should see the house first,' Victor said.

'Plenty of time for that,' Margery said.

'What about the wedding night?' Walter said, leering.

'That isn't for us,' said Margery. 'We're going to play father and mother when I move to the house, but nothing else.'

'I don't mind you speaking so bluntly in Walter's presence,' said Victor with his customary dignity, 'because we can trust Walter, but never in anybody else's presence. We owe that to David.'

'I owe David nothing,' she said full of bitterness.

'The child,' laughed Walter.

'I don't appreciate the joke,' said Victor.

'Sorry,' Walter said. 'You ought to ask me to lunch.'

'I'll ask you,' said Victor.

The forgotten woman had left already, the three of them

146

were still standing outside the town hall. It was Margery who made the first move by saying, 'I'm off, but I'll be in touch with you Victor, very soon.'

On her way back to Paris she wondered whether Victor would play. She wasn't altogether certain, for he looked like one who never tired of playing the part he had chosen. In Paris Mme Hermine didn't stop pointing out to her that they should take all the advantage they could of her possessing an English husband, especially as the husband was penniless. A fortnight later Margery arrived at the White House. (The Cokes came to the neighbourhood only five years afterwards.) Margery found Victor in overalls, whitewashing the walls of the hall. Everything was in a dilapidated state, and what little furniture there was she considered an eyesore.

'I must say,' she said, 'David palmed you off with a dud one. This house will collapse on you.'

'How can you say that?' said Victor, looking hurt. She had noticed he had the knack of looking hurt. 'This house is my dream. I'll turn it into a beauty. Anyway, in five years' time I'll have the farm, and that should keep us in ease.'

'How will you manage during the five years?'

'David said he would help a bit.'

'I'm not too keen on David's help.'

'We owe this house to him.'

'We owe it to the unborn child,' she laughed.

'Margery,' he said severely, 'we must begin to live up to what David expects from us in return for this princely gift.'

'Princely gift,' she mocked, pointing at the peeling ceiling.

'It is a princely gift, and we both accepted his conditions.'

He wouldn't play, the pompous fool he was, she said to herself.

'I can still walk out on you both, Victor.'

'Don't do that,' he said quickly. 'I don't want David to consider me a cad, a man without honour.'

'In that case you'll have to listen to me. Furthermore, you'll be able to make good money, and get this house repaired without having to starve till the farm is yours.'

'I'd do anything reasonable to get this house repaired as it deserves. And there's the garden. I haven't even started on it.'

'It's bloody cold in here,' she said. 'I kept the taxi waiting. We'll go to some pub in Folkestone, where I'll tell you what I want from you in your own interest.'

'I'll make a fire in the study, it's small, so it'll warm up in a few minutes. Send the taxi away. I'll make a fire in one of the bedrooms for you, too. Stay the night. You must accustom yourself to living here.'

'Pray, what will we eat?'

'I've got eggs and corned beef.'

'And what will we drink?'

'No drinks here, too expensive.'

'I'll go in the taxi to get some whisky and wine, and when I'm back I'll send it away. To live here you need a car.'

'A car? I haven't money enough to buy paint for the walls.'

'You'll be able to if you do what I want.'

On her way to the village she was still uncertain whether he would play. On her way back she became convinced that he would. The man was in love with the White House, which she considered a horror. He had married her to get the house, was willing to play the part of the father of another man's son, in short he would do anything for the house. She smiled at him confidently as he took her into the study, where a coal fire burned, the only furniture a deck chair and a kitchen chair. He motioned her to the deck chair.

'This room needs decent furniture,' she said.

'Don't rub it in, I'm doing all I can.'

'You'll have to do more than that. Give me a whisky.'

She watched him as he poured out two whiskies. He was definitely good looking, yet she had seldom seen a man who left her so indifferent. Wouldn't it be a glorious revenge on David to fall in love with Victor and live with him happy ever after? However, she was too experienced to believe in such easy revenge. The repulsion she felt for him was striking proof of it. 'Listen to me,' she said.

'I'm all ears.'

'In Paris I work for and am associated with a Mme Hermine, who keeps a bar near the Madeleine, a district frequented by expensive women, if you take my meaning.' Victor nodded. 'Many of them, and others, too, come to the bar to pick up men, naturally for purely financial reasons.' Victor nodded again. A serious fool, she thought. 'One whom we know well came over to London, and when she came on a visit to Paris she looked us up, and painted an alluring picture of London. Listening to her I couldn't help thinking that the whole male population of London was dying to go to bed with French girls and hang the expense. I checked on it. She wasn't exaggerating. Mme Hermine has an admirable business sense. Moreover, she has a large female acquaintance. Her idea is to send French girls over, have somebody here to keep an eye on them, and be paid for the trouble she took and will go on taking. As I'm on the Paris end of the business we need somebody at the London end. The person we have in mind is you. With the share that will be yours you'll be able to repair this house, and live here in the state you want to and which the house deserves.'

While she spoke her eyes hadn't left him. He listened gravely, he was truly all ears, and she was sure that he would have listened with the same serious expression if she were offering to let him run the country.

'This house deserves everything I can give it,' he said. 'Tell me honestly, are those women free agents?'

'What do you mean by free agents?'

'I've read about white slave traffic.'

'Oh that,' she said. 'I don't know about other people, but I can assure you that the women Mme Hermine and I have in mind are simply dying to come over here. There are a lot of them who'd never prostituted themselves in their lives. One of their first reactions when we spoke to them was that their families wouldn't know about it if they earned their living in that manner in faraway England, where nobody could recognise them. Many don't dare to stand at Paris street corners for fear that some cousin from Brittany might run into them. London is anonymous, back home they can continue playing the virtuous woman they all want to think they are.'

'Exactly what is it you ask of me?'

'Mme Hermine has a business connection in London, a Miss Hulbert, who has a large house which she has turned into a maison de rendez-vous, and she can find all the clients she wants. Being a procuress in her own way, Mme Hermine doesn't trust other procuresses. Therefore, she needs a controller, and if you want to make money accept that job. You'll find out from the girls how much they receive from clients, from Miss Hulbert how much the girls earn, so you'll be able to check and figure out how much they really earn, and if you can't Mme Hermine and I will work it out.'

'I'm good with figures,' said Victor, almost offended.

'You'll keep an eye on the girls, which is easy enough. Your French is passable, you can take them out now and then, make them talk, see Miss Hulbert from time to time, and most important when they arrive in London you find them lodgings and keep a check on their remaining there.'

'And if one of them suddenly walks out on the . . . organisation.'

'You'll let us know. As they'll all come over owing us money we'll have the whiphand. Something else that's very important. Immediately on arrival in London the girls must marry Englishmen.'

'What on earth for?'

'If they marry Englishmen they can't be deported. If you catch a foreign woman whoring she's deported at once. Such husbands – you can imagine the trash they are – can be found for a hundred pounds. The money which we advance is paid to the husbands on leaving the registry office. Then the couples part for good. You'll find husbands, very easily.'

'Sorry, Margery,' said Victor, 'but I won't do that. I don't mix with scum, I can't stand the riff-raff.'

'How finicky you are,' she said, wanting to add that needing a hundred pounds or needing a house was similar.

She was too intelligent to annoy a person from whom she needed something.

'For this house I'm willing to do all that you ask except mix with the scum that finding such husbands would entail. But I've the solution for you. Walter. The poor chap is so broke that he'll jump at it. He's a very good mixer.'

'That's an idea. We'll contact him tomorrow.'

Margery lit a fresh cigarette, ran a little hot water to warm up the bath, then returned to her first night in the White House.

She went to bed pleased with the results. Victor had made a fire in the bedroom she had chosen, and heaped so much coal on it that she had to open the window. An owl hooted, the pale moon cast her feeble beams down on the flat landscape. She shuddered, and decided to spend as little time as she could in that house. There was no key to the door, and as she lay down she wondered whether Victor would make any effort to get his wife to do her duty. She hoped not, because she didn't want to ruffle his conceit before he started working for Mme Hermine and her. Victor never came.

Walter indeed jumped at it, and a fortnight later Margery arrived at Victoria Station with a red-haired girl from Picardy called Evelyne. Victor met them at the station, and with his exquisite manners and distinguished presence he made Evelyne feel immediately at home in London. When she saw the first policeman she cried out, 'Regardez, un Bobbie,' and her joy was complete. The next day she met her future husband.

'Couldn't you have found a less repulsive man, Walter?' Margery laughed.

The following night she spent at the White House as she was taking ship to Boulogne-sur-Mer the next morning. Before they went to their separate rooms on the first floor she gave Victor a sum large enough to repaint all the walls. They had drunk a fair amount of whisky, and under its soothing influence Victor became loquacious, and told her the story of his life. He was born in Berkshire in a house larger than the White House. His father hunted, shot and fished, and when his own father, the very rich man, died they moved to his manor in Wiltshire. Victor was eight years old at the time of his mother's death. His father, who had been a spendthrift all his adult life, added women to his hunting, shooting and fishing. He got properly caught by one on whom he lavished most of his dwindling fortune, and gave her the house in Berkshire. 'Can you imagine that, Margery? The house I was born in.' The father died of a surfeit of love soon after the war broke out, leaving his son a pile of debts. Victor joined up, and didn't feel the pinch till the war was won and he left the Army. During one of his leaves he went down to Berkshire and stood outside the gate to gape at the house he was born in. He saw an enormous woman in her thirties walking in the garden, talking to a man who looked like a gardener.

'What did you do?' Margery asked.

'I left in disgust with tears in my eyes.'

'In your place I'd have introduced myself and tried to make friends with her.'

'Never. She was a usurper. That house should have been mine. She stole it from me. I went back once more, and heard in the village that she had sold it and gone to live in London.'

'Now you have this house, so it all ended well.'

'It resembles Willow House. It was called Willow House because of the willows beside the stream. When David brought me here I felt as if I had come home, were back in my own.'

That explains everything, said Margery to herself.

'Keep an eye on Evelyne and Miss Hulbert,' she said in the morning. 'Soon you'll have a car.'

Her child was born in a Dover nursing home, a boy with David's eyes. 'We should call him Claud,' said Victor. She asked why. 'My grandfather was called Claud, and he was such a grand man.' That should have warned her, but at the time all she thought of was that since she refused to give him the name of David he could be called by any name Victor wanted. 'He must be baptised into the Holy Apostolic

152

Church,' was Victor's next decision. 'I'm a pretty bad Catholic, but my forebears were all Catholics, and I can't betray them.' As religion was a blank to her she let him have his way.

'Your son's on the line,' called Sylvie.

'Tell him to come to lunch,' Margery called back.

As she had to go frequently to Paris they took a nurse for Claud, an Irishwoman with hair like barbed wire. During her stays in the White House Margery watched fascinated as Victor became in his eyes and mind Claud's father. When the boy was two nobody could have persuaded him that he wasn't his offspring. One day she observed, 'He has the same smile as David.'

'He has my smile,' Victor quietly said.

To let a lie conquer truth nauseated her. By the time Claud was five Victor was completely the self-made father. When Claud had mumps, Victor rang her in Paris and, on arriving at the White House, she found him in tears. He was the sick-nurse, spending his nights looking into the sick-room every few minutes, and in the daytime he moaned, 'My poor son, my poor son.' She felt like vomiting. Shortly after Claud's recovery Lil appeared on the scene, a great relief to Margery who came over less and less. On her rare visits she saw her son turning into a complete stranger. David and I were the parents, she said to herself, till Victor took over. Now the boy is completely his. We've nothing more to do with him. The three of them seated at the dining-room table, served by Lil who sat down with them afterwards, were father, son and a visitor. 'Don't you think I look like father?' Claud used to ask her, and Victor calmly waited for her to say he was the image of him.

Margery got out of the bath. How depressing such memories are, she said to the glass. After them she bloody well needed a man. It would have to be Michel since at a moment's notice she couldn't get hold of any other.

'There's too much light on the Riviera,' said Mrs Coke on the morning Ludmilla started out for Cannes, 'so wear dark glasses.'

As the aircraft rose from the airfield, and she had opened the magazine her father had bought for her, she asked herself what Claud was doing at that moment. She hadn't warned him of her coming. Let the delicious surprise be complete. She would walk into the hotel, ask for his room number, then go up, knock on the door, he would ask who it was, and she would say, 'Ludmilla, my darling Claud,' open the door, and fall into his arms, though calmly and gently so that he should understand there was no room for monkey tricks. Let them come after the wedding bells had been rung.

At that very moment there was a knock on Claud's bedroom door.

'Who is it?' he called, thinking it could only be David. However, it was nine, and David wouldn't be up yet.

'Mme Romei,' said Mme Romei. 'I must have a word with you, monsieur. It brooks no delay.'

'Come in, madame,' said Claud who was already dressed.

Mme Romei stamped into the bedroom, her cheeks flushed, anger bursting from her dark eyes. She closed the door, then leaned against it.

'Monsieur, I must ask you to leave my hotel at once.'

'Why, madame? I like it a lot here.'

'I can well understand that you like it here, another reason to ask you to leave.'

She had worked herself into total fury, reminding Claud of a toad he had disturbed once.

'Frankly, I don't understand you,' he said.

'My niece, who's a depraved creature, came to your room the other night. Don't deny it. One of my oldest clients saw her entering your room, then he heard noises I prefer not to think about.'

That client could only be Rudge.

'Madame,' said Claud, trying to strike the attitude of the

faithful lover and the protector of the damsel in distress, 'Modeste had every reason to come here. We're going to get married as soon as we can.'

Mme Romei nearly collapsed, yet had enough strength left to lean forward as if she were hard of hearing and hadn't got the meaning of his words.

'What did you say?' she asked in a hoarse voice.

'I said Modeste and I are getting married. We love each other, and when we go to England Marie-Bénédicte will come with us.'

Mme Romei underwent another change as she straightened herself, turning into the proprietress of a two-star hotel and two blocks of flats in Nice, a proprietress who had to defend her properties against any adventurer. This one would vanish, as had the student, and if in nine months time Modeste pushed out another child it couldn't do more harm than the first one had caused. Surely she wasn't the only well-to-do virtuous aunt whose niece had one bastard after the other.

'Modeste,' she said, 'is of age, therefore I can't stop her from marrying whomever she wants, but I must make it very clear to you, monsieur, that she won't get a centime from me, no dowry, no trousseau, in short nothing. And it's useless waiting for an inheritance.'

'Madame,' said Claud the man of means. 'We don't need anything. My father, who died recently and who was the finest man I knew, left me enough to be able to support Modeste and her child. I have a house, a farm, cattle and pigs, also some sheep, so I can keep a wife in reasonable comfort.' He was proud of himself. He had spoken modestly as befits a man of means.

'Monsieur,' said Mme Romei. 'This changes everything. Could you do me the favour of waiting till noon?'

'Waiting for what, may I ask?'

'To continue the discussion. I leave you, but I'll be in my little salon which is beyond the writing-room at twelve sharp. Come in without knocking.'

She bowed, then went from the room. Modeste was in the hall already.

'My dear child,' said **Mme Romei** in fluted tones, 'do me the favour of driving to Cimiez, see the concierge of my house, and tell her to send me the rent book which I haven't seen this month. I'll pay for the petrol.'

Modeste gave her aunt an astonished look, for she hadn't seen her so amiable before. She's out of the way, said Mme Romei to herself. The rent book, as a matter of fact, was in the drawer of her desk. She waited patiently till eleven, when she rang David. 'What's that?' he asked in an abrupt voice that meant she had woken him up.

'Mme Romei speaking. I hope I didn't wake you, M. David.'

'You did. What is it?'

'Could I have a word with you? It's somewhat urgent.'

'For you or for me?'

'Oh, you guess everything, M. David,' she cooed. 'For me. When can I see you? I'll come to your room if you prefer. Anyway, one can chat there better than in the hall, where the walls have ears.'

'Come up in twenty minutes' time.'

When the twenty minutes were up she summoned one of the chambermaids, whom she told to sit behind the desk while she was upstairs. She knocked more gently on David's door than she had on Claud's. He was sitting on the bed, wearing a navy blue silk dressing-gown. My beau ideal, she sighed.

'What is it, madame?'

'You know M. Darnell well? I mean his circumstances.' David nodded. 'He's well off, so he told me.'

Being nobody's fool David said, 'He's quite well off. Has a house and a large farm. I'm sure he's a hard worker. Besides, I'll remember him in my will, and it won't be a small legacy.'

'You have no idea how happy you made me, M. David. The dear young man came to me this morning to ask for the hand of my dear Modeste.'

'Excellent,' said David. 'May I congratulate you? You'll find him a first class nephew-in-law.' Victor, he thought, would have been shocked by his son wanting to marry a foreigner.

'Thank you, monsieur,' said Mme Romei, grasping his hand. 'You're such an old friend that I can talk to you freely. After Modeste's little mishap I had fears she wouldn't find the sort of husband I want for her. So I'm doubly pleased. That courageous girl has confessed everything to your young friend.'

'How did he react?'

'He took it like a real English gentleman. When they marry they'll take my little grandniece to England.'

'Good,' said David, wondering whether Claud would start pretending that the baby was his.

'The wedding will take place here in Cannes. You're cordially invited to it.'

'Thank you, madame. I'll have to think of a suitable wedding present for Modeste. I've known her most of her life.'

'She's very fond of you, M. David,' said Mme Romei, her cup of happiness brimming over. 'Thank you again for the information.'

At twelve sharp she was seated in her little salon, which resembled a dentist's waiting room. An engraving of Napoleon at the battle of Marengo hung above the door.

'Ah, here you are, monsieur,' she said, rising as Claud came in.

'Where's Modeste?' he asked.

'I sent her on a business errand to Nice, but she's sure to be back before lunch. Tonight I'll take you and Modeste out to dinner to celebrate your engagement. Perhaps your mother would care to join us? And would you like me to invite M. David too?'

'I'm lunching with my mother. I'll tell her. I'm sure she'll be delighted to come. Please ask M. David. I'm very fond of him.'

Margery was the only dark spot on Mme Romei's luminous horizon. Would she have to see a lot of that woman whose reputation wasn't too good? Anyway, she could pretend she knew nothing about it. Besides, Alice's London Bar earned good money.

'I was only joking when I was in your room. I wouldn't let my niece, whom I brought up like a loving mother, go to England in rags. I'll provide her with a costly trousseau, and as a wedding present I'll give her one or two of my jewels. And I can tell you now that you've become a member of the family that she's my sole surviving relation. You know what that means in the long run.'

Before he could think of what to answer he heard Modeste asking the chambermaid where her aunt was. Then she came flying in, the prettiest sight Claud ever had seen, saying in the doorway, 'The concierge swears she posted the rent book on the fifth.' She saw Claud, blushed to her ears, her eyes saying she couldn't make out the situation.

'M. Darnell, whom from now on I'll call Claud,' said Mme Romei, 'has asked your hand in marriage. I gladly agreed to your marrying him. I congratulate you, my well beloved niece, on having chosen such an excellent young man, a true English gentleman.'

'You're too good, my aunt,' gushed Modeste.

'I think I'll leave you alone a little,' said the generous aunt. 'Offer your fiancé any aperitif he wants. Accompany me to my desk, Claud.' From the door she called, 'I won't keep him, my little Modeste.' On reaching the desk she whispered, 'Promise not to tell her about my visit to your room, and how I found out about you two.'

'I promise.'

'It is a good thing to start married life with a secret or two,' smiled Mme Romei.

'I just can't believe it,' said Modeste on his return.

'You have to. I told you there was no cause to worry.'

'I ought to be ashamed of myself,' said Modeste after their third embrace, 'because I didn't believe that my aunt could be so generous.'

'You're late, Claud,' said Margery when he arrived.

'Because he has something to tell you,' said David.

'So you know,' said Claud.

'Mme Romei came to my room to tell me,' said David.

'What's the mystery?' asked Margery.

'Mother, I'm going to marry Modeste Romei.'

'Who is she?' asked Margery.

'The niece of our hotel-keeper.'

'Oh yes, I've seen her once. Has rather fascinating eyes. When will you marry her?'

She ought to show a little more interest, said David to himself.

'As soon as possible,' said Claud. 'Wish me luck, mother.'

'Le déjeuner est servi,' said Sylvie from the door.

'I wish you luck, Claud,' said Margery, starting for the dining-room. She was a little taken aback as Claud stopped her to kiss her on the cheek. Her sudden movement didn't escape David.

Over the carbonade Claud spoke of Mme Romei's invitation to dinner.

'Can't I get out of it?' Margery said.

'You can't,' snapped David. 'Tell Mme Romei that your mother and I are delighted, and we both will be at the hotel at eight.'

Margery smiled to herself.

Claud was the first to leave, and on his way down the stairs he exulted at the thought of he and Modeste being able to smile at each other in public. He wasn't born to lead a secret life.

'You behaved abominably,' said David to Margery after Claud had gone.

'And you make me laugh. He's as much your son as mine.'

'I behave as well as the circumstances allow me.'

'The circumstances created by your ambition. At least I admit I'm Claud's mother. Oh, I say, we all forgot about Ludmilla. What will Claud say to her?'

'I'm sure he's going to ask my advice.'

'The useful father. I must ask you to leave, Papa David. I'm expecting a guest.'

'Who's the guest?'

'Michel.'

'You said you'd finished with him.'

'I did finish with him, this afternoon is an exception.'

'See you in the bar,' said David, 'and for God's sake behave yourself tonight.'

'I'll do my best, Papa David.'

She was in bed with Michel when Ludmilla rang the door bell. She found Cannes bewildering. How right her mother was about the light, and already she longed for the pastel colours of Sussex. It had been Mrs Coke's advice to call first on Mrs Darnell, advice which Ludmilla had decided to disregard. However, in that alien town on the move she felt so much in need of her mother's protection that she went straight to Margery. She lives above a bar, she said to herself on getting out of the taxi. Neither she nor her mother were aware of Claud's mother's keeping a bar. Victor would never have told them for a man of quality like himself could have a wife living in the South of France, because the English climate was too harsh for her, that she should run a bar was beneath his image of himself.

'Can I see Mrs Darnell?' asked Margery.

'Mademoiselle, je ne comprends pas l'anglais,' said Sylvie.

'Ah. Madame Darnell, s'il vous plaît.'

'Elle est sortie,' said Sylvie, her answer when Margery had a man with her. If she were out she said, 'Madame n'est pas là.'

Ludmilla left, and she had to ask several people to direct her before she found the Hôtel Romei. A youngish-looking man sat behind the large desk, one Didier, whom Mme Romei had called in as she and Modeste were both out for the afternoon. Mme Romei had gone to an old cronie of hers to tell her of the admirable match Modeste was making. Surely, thought Ludmilla, he spoke English.

'Which is Mr Darnell's room number?' she asked.

Didier examined the list of the hotel guests, then glanced up and saw the key hanging in the company of many others. This was not the hour for hotel guests to be in, with the one exception of Rudge, who sat scowling in the writing-room.

'Say, he ain't in,' said Didier in his best American.

'When do you expect him back?' she asked crestfallen. Her grand entry into his bedroom wouldn't take place.

'Say, dunno,' said Didier.

'I'll wait for him. Where can I wait for him?'

'In there. Okay.'

She took her fair hair, white skin and blue eyes into the writing-room.

'You're English of course,' said Rudge.

'That's not difficult to guess,' said Ludmilla, sitting down with her back to him. She had a horror of strangers, and didn't care for the looks of Rudge.

'Staying here?' he asked her back.

'I'm not.'

'Then what are you doing here?'

'Waiting for a friend.' She unfolded *The Times*. 'Excuse me, but I hadn't time to look at it in the plane.'

'Oh, you flew out today.'

She didn't answer, and began to read but without taking in what she read.

'I'm living here,' said Rudge after a while. 'There's no room left for men of my ilk in England. I was provincial commissioner in Kenya in our lost imperial days.' The back didn't move. 'Is the friend you're waiting for staying in this hotel?'

'He is,' she said, not wanting to be too rude.

'I know everybody here. What's his name?'

Her first reaction was to say none of your business. The man was old, however, and she was sure that neither of her parents would approve of straightforward rudeness. 'Claud Darnell,' she said, burying her face in the newspaper.

'Claud Darnell. I know him, know him perhaps too well.'

'What do you mean by knowing him perhaps too well?' she asked, turning round.

'It means I have a very poor opinion of him.'

'I don't care a rap about your opinion. We're engaged to be married.'

Her voice showed her anger. Unperturbed, Rudge came over to her table, pulled up a chair, and sat down opposite her. 'You must break off the engagement,' he said.

'It's none of your business,' she said, sure now that her parents wouldn't disapprove of her.

'It is my business, dear young lady,' said Rudge. 'I'm an old-fashioned man, which means a man of principle. You look a decent young person, we belong to the same world, therefore it's my duty to warn you.'

'Warn me about what?' she asked, beginning to feel helpless, as though her strength had snapped. Why wasn't her mother there to protect her?

'Claud Darnell, it is my duty to tell you, has a young woman in bed with him every night. I know the young woman, a shameless creature.'

'Stop it,' cried Ludmilla, but couldn't resist asking, 'How do you know that?'

'I didn't see her going into his room, but passing his door I heard the animal noises they made. Alas, unmistakable. I'm sure my instinct told me that I'd meet and save you. I waited behind my door, waited for hours, to see her emerge from his room. She came out at six in the morning, lust written all over her face.'

Ludmilla was bordering on collapse. Her innocent little brother made animal noises, no better than a billy-goat. She couldn't marry a billy-goat, she wasn't depraved. Some horrible blown-up tart reeking of lust shared those animal noises with him. She could never look at him again. She recollected his wanting to touch her breasts and the many times he had tried to put his hand up her leg. Once a billy-goat always a billy-goat, the bigger fool she for not having seen it long ago. Was there a plane this evening to London? She must get back to her mother.

'Well, thank you,' she said, and walked out of the hotel.

Rudge looked after her, regretting her going. He should have led up to it more slowly. He went into the hall to have a chat with Didier. 'I've got to write out bills,' said Didier, who couldn't stick him. None-the-less, Rudge remained in the hall and was still there when Claud and Modeste came back.

'Mr Rudge,' said Claud, 'we're both grateful to you for

having been the first to tell Mme Romei that Modeste and I are getting married.' So far so good and praiseworthy, but Rudge's angry flush was too hard to bear. 'You old sneak.'

'You deserve a whipping,' said Rudge, stamping out of the hotel.

Claud went upstairs to write to Ludmilla.

Two mornings later the Cokes were breakfasting, in mild sunshine. Mr Coke was talking, Mrs Coke nodded her approval. He explained to Ludmilla that she had been too rash, too intolerant. She would be entitled to feel outraged if she had shared her bed with Claud. Young men weren't abstemious nowadays, she had old-fashioned virtues that didn't fit into the times they lived in, and as Ludmilla smiled at her father, waiting to be convinced, Gretchen brought in Claud's letter. Ludmilla tore the envelope open. In the first sentence Claud announced his engagement to Modeste, in the second that he would return only after the wedding, and ended his brief letter, 'We must remain friends. After all we were only friends ever since we met.'

Dirty billy-goat, Ludmilla said to herself.

4

After Mme Romei's dinner party David felt as heavy as if he had eaten bricks, the fault of neither the food nor Mme Romei. It was Margery's attitude, a mixture of aloofness and boredom, that had turned the evening into sheer hell, his sole hope being that Mme Romei was too pleased with herself to notice it. And Claud? In his total bliss he probably hadn't. David didn't accompany Margery to Alice's London Bar, for to see Elfrida would only add to the heaviness within him. He walked back to the hotel and passing the all-night café, he saw Nelly through the open door, but he hadn't the strength left even for her. On entering the hall he heard voices in the salon. Recognising Mme Romei's and Claud's he dived into the lift.

He hadn't been back so early for ages. It was no good

trying to sleep. He sat down in the armchair, poured out a stiff whisky, and his thoughts, waiting for their chance during dinner, rushed him back to the young MP he had been.

Jessica was as perfect a wife as any ambitious politician could wish for. With her at his side he saw a long vista of success, and true enough at the General Election of 1950 he was re-elected with an increased majority. Labour couldn't hold out long, there were bound to be new elections, and when the Conservatives were back in their own the powers that be wouldn't overlook him. Of that, Jessica's uncle was as sure as he. The Margery affair had been settled perfectly. After his last visit to Paris he hadn't heard any more from her, which he couldn't help regretting. Yet he had to admit that it was better like that. Victor had written once, sending the letter to the House. He told him that everything was going well, that he wouldn't recognise the White House, but making no mention of the child. David wrote back to say in the circumstances he felt it was preferable not to correspond, let each of them continue going his way. He never heard from Victor again.

Apart from watching over David and his parliamentary career, Jessica's fervent wish was to have children. Bearing them would show that she wasn't quite useless as a woman. She didn't become pregnant. Shortly after the 1950 General Election she went to consult a specialist to find out why she couldn't have children. He sent her to another, and after several different tests she forced the truth out of him, namely that she had leukaemia, which had of course nothing to do with the object she had in mind when she went to the doctors. She looked at medical books, and perceived she hadn't long to live, but she said not a word to David. If he said, 'You don't look well,' or, 'You don't eat enough,' Jessica said it was a cold or indigestion.

However, she began to sink fast as if life had tired of her, and he heard the truth, or rather, she couldn't keep it from him any longer. He was miserable and heartbroken, for he had come to cherish and admire her, also to rely on her. A pathetic scene took place in the hospital, where she was approaching death. 'You're too young, David,' she said, 'to go through life alone. You must marry again.'

'Never, darling. You're my only wife for ever and ever.'

She cried for the first time, a lament more for him than for herself.

Lifting the glass of whisky David saw the hospital room with emaciated Jessica lying on the bed, her face so sunk that her eyes seemed too large for it. He emptied the glass, and poured out more whisky.

She died, and he gave her a grand funeral. Alone back in Brinworth Hall he thought that the only way he could show Jessica that her memory couldn't die was to make a triumphant career in Parliament. Without his yet realising it, she had taken that career to the grave with her. In the same year the Conservatives triumphed in the General Election David lost his seat to a Liberal who got a majority of six. After the recount he admitted to himself that he had been beaten, though not by his opponent but by himself.

Looking back on it twenty years afterwards he saw nothing wrong in his despair at that time. He had married Jessica with a political career in mind, they had lived harmoniously together and fortune shone on them. The sun of fortune set with her death; thus, throwing his hand in was all that was left. It had been as much a physical as a mental procedure. His body couldn't take what his mind had ceased to accept. Both wanted to run, to escape for ever, and in their solidarity they rejected his dreams. He was rich enough to stand aside, no financial necessity could force him to change his mind. He could go, therefore he would.

He saw his solicitors, arranged for Brinworth Hall to be handed over to a charity Jessica had been interested in, and for part of his income to be used by them, too. The estate agent should do his best as long as he was left in peace, and when he looked for the last time at his vast house he thanked God that he wouldn't have to spend another night in it. He motored to London, stayed in his flat, but after the first twenty-four hours he felt like being in a prison. He must move on.

He saw Jessica's uncle in his club from which he was going to resign. He made it clear to him that he wouldn't try again.

'You're not the first MP who lost his seat,' said the uncle. 'You've done so well in the House that a constituency will easily be found for you.'

'I don't want to go back.'

'Why don't you?'

'I can't explain it even to myself.'

The evening after David was in Paris.

As he walked to Mme Hermine's bar, neither could he explain why he wanted to see Margery. To fall into her arms, to forget in them the years that had separated him from her didn't even occur to him. He was on his way to Margery because he was on his way to her. He opened the door, his eyes waiting for the sight of her. The red curtains were gone, the pink lampshades too. The dark blue wall paper had been changed to yellow, and behind the bar stood two barmen, complete strangers to him. The clientele was mostly male, the few women were soberly elegant, wives of some of the male customers taking a drink before going out to dinner or to a theatre, or perhaps to a concert. David addressed the taller of the two barmen, a man with an infinitely sad countenance.

'Is Mme Hermine in?'

'You mean Mme Dupuis?'

'I didn't know her family name. I used to be a customer here. She was on the fat side, and wore many rings.'

'That's Mme Dupuis,' said the barman, and David appreciated that with Mme Hermine turning into Mme Dupuis he had ceased to be in the place where he had known Margery. 'She sold out. The new proprietor is a M. Guénault. We cleaned up this place a bit.'

'I can see that. You don't know where she is?'

'I don't, monsieur. What will you take?'

'A dry Martini,' said David, and perceiving that he was dealing with a decent customer the barman promised to ask M. Guénault on the telephone. M. Guénault seldom came to the bar.

After David's second dry Martini the barman telephoned.

Mme Hermine had retired to Cannes, but her partner, a Mme Darnell, kept a bar there called Alice's London Bar.

'Thank you,' said David. 'Cannes is a very long way from here.'

'You surely noticed that this bar is much better run since we took over, and the clientele is very different, too.'

One more reason not to come again, thought David as he left.

That night he picked up a moderately good looking woman in a night club, took her to his hotel, and when she left after dawn he felt the same about her as about the bar that had been Mme Hermine's. Not what he was looking for. He shrugged his shoulders because he had no idea what he was looking for. In fact, was he looking for anything?

Next night he travelled in the Blue Train to Cannes. It was the end of November yet the sun shone gaily. He left his luggage at the station as he had no plans. He might move on to Nice or Monte Carlo. He sauntered along the streets, vaguely intending to go to the Croisette. Later he would look for Alice's London Bar in the telephone directory. He took a street to the left, another to the right, and in front of him he saw in large letters, Alice's London Bar. That's funny, he thought.

In those days Margery was in the bar from ten in the morning onward, no getting up late and wallowing in her bath yet. Her tall figure was like a poplar in a flat field, and even before reaching the bar he saw she had gained in self-assurance.

'God, you've changed,' she said as if she had seen him only a few weeks ago.

'It isn't surprising. How are you, Margery?'

'How did you find this place?'

'I went to the bar in Paris, where they gave me the address.'

'I bought it eight months ago. Mme Hermine has retired, has a villa in Super-Cannes. She put up part of the money. So you're an MP no more.'

'I thought you don't know or care what goes on in England.'

'I was at the White House with my husband and child

during the General Election.' Her voice was rasping. 'As it's your first visit here have a drink on the house.'

'That's awfully decent of you. I'll have a pastis.'

'Where's your wife?'

'So you don't know all that goes on or doesn't in England.'

'I don't understand what you mean. Are you divorced?'

'My wife died.'

'And you lost at the elections. You'd better have a double pastis, poor David.'

'Thank you, Margery. You can gloat. All my dreams are shattered.'

'We're quits then because my dreams were shattered, too.' A man with an RAF moustache came in. 'We can't talk here. He's English.' She turned to the man. 'Hullo, Mac.'

'Hullo, Marge, some French beer, please.'

'Can you lunch with me?' David asked.

'I must stay here. We're very busy at lunch time.'

'What about dinner?'

'That's the busiest time.'

'Marge is the busiest woman in the whole of the South of France,' said Mac.

'Thanks, Mac,' she said.

'Find time for a chat,' said David, ignoring Mac as he would ignore scores of others.

'Are you staying in Cannes?' she asked.

'Don't know yet.'

'My barmaid comes at two. If you're here at, say, half-past two, we can talk.' She dropped her voice. 'But have we anything to say to each other?'

'We'll see,' he said.

He went down to the Croisette, blinked in the sunshine, then booked a room in the Carlton, and an hour later he was back in Alice's London Bar.

David poured out more whisky. He heard the lift stop at his floor, then two voices, both male, talking on their way to the room at the end of the passage. His new relationship with Margery must have begun when he returned to Alice's London Bar.

168

'It's too early,' she said.

'I'll have a sandwich in lieu of lunch.'

'Rillettes, ham, pâté or cheese?'

'Rillettes,' he said, 'and some wine.'

'Beaujolais, Bordeaux or Côte de Provence?'

'Let it be Côte de Provence.'

A sickly-looking waiter served him at a table facing the counter. He had only glimpses of Margery because of the crowd that hid her. She was the life and soul of the gathering; her voice and laughter dominated, and the customers ate out of her hand. Now and then their eyes met, but he couldn't make out what went on behind those eyes. Mac wasn't in the crowd. He felt a strange sort of peace descending on him. He couldn't even be certain that he could call it peace. Perhaps it had some other name which in twenty long years he hadn't managed to hit on. None-the-less, he felt more relaxed than he had since Jessica's death and no need to torture himself. The barmaid who arrived at two was the spit of the women he used to see in Mme Hermine's bar. So Margery was still in the trade.

The crowd had thinned out, and at half past two only a few customers were left, two of them girls who sat on barstools in deadly boredom. They too reminded him of the Madeleine neighbourhood. Margery came over, the barmaid following with two brandies.

'It sickens me to see you having to work so hard,' David said.

'I love it, and I'm making good money. Besides, I don't need money. Victor and I are in business together.'

'What sort of business?'

'Guess.'

'I didn't expect that from Victor.'

'From me, of course, you expected it. Haven't we met in Pigalle?'

'Don't be unkind, Margery. What I wanted to get at and what I had already proposed to you is that I have more money than I can use, my needs have shrunk with my downfall, therefore you can chuck this bar and live on the fat of the land.'

'That's where we came in, I mean went out.'

'The first thing you said when I came in was that I had changed. Margery, I'm very different from the man I was when we came in.'

'I'm a very different woman, too. When I think of the utter faith I had in you, I laugh at myself as nobody will ever laugh at me. Whenever I thought of you, which I did every ten minutes, I saw us in the bedroom in the rue des Capucines, you outlining your plan, a plan you had evolved because you didn't trust me. When you'd explained it you got on top of me because that's all I'm good for. Yet I still love you, but it's a love that has no substance left. It's loving because I loved so completely. It was the greatest experience of my life. I love you because you gave me that experience. One can't repeat the same. I'd have gone on with you even if you'd come to Paris only once a year. I'd have brought up your son happily because with him beside me you wouldn't ever have been absent, even if we met rarely. But you killed it that morning. Married to somebody else, I couldn't blackmail you or your wife. If I refused to marry, the refusal proved I intended to blackmail.'

'Stop it, Margery.'

'I'm speaking the truth. I don't really care for my son because he reminds me of that morning. Victor has persuaded himself that the child is his, and if I said it was yours he'd remind me that we accepted him as the father, and it would be unfair on you to say it was yours. That's where we stand, my one-time David. I know how lonely and wretched you are now, so come here as often as you want. I'll always be happy to see you, but that's all.'

'Couldn't we . . .'

'You know as well as I do that we couldn't. Now I'm going upstairs to my flat, where my lover of the moment is waiting for me. Come back if you want to at eight o'clock and dine in the flat.'

'Thank you, I'll be back.'

He dined with her in the flat, and when they went down to

the bar, which was full of females, he said in order to see her reaction, 'I wouldn't mind a bash tonight. Whom do you recommend?'

'Ursule,' Margery called to a dark haired girl sitting on a bar stool, filing her nails. The girl came promptly. 'Ursule, I want to recommend this monsieur to you. He couldn't be nicer.' She turned to him, and said in English, 'Which is true in a sense.'

Next morning he was back in Alice's London Bar.

David emptied his glass, and listened to the quiet of the hotel. He washed the glass under the tap in the bathroom. He hated to see a dirty glass. He walked to the all-night café in search of Nelly. She wasn't present. He had two whiskies, and felt he was strong enough to face sleep. On his way back to the hotel he remembered Margery's behaviour at dinner. He hadn't the right to be annoyed with her.

He had to wake the night porter to get his key.

VII

I

In the aeroplane Walter had a sudden fit of anger. Such fits took a lot out of him, as he was wont to complain to Nicole, the usual cause of them. This time it was Margery. For no reason he could explain he remembered the one and only pass he had made at her while they were in business together. She had brought over a girl from Paris, he already had a husband ready for her, and having won at the races, which happened to him but rarely, he was in an expansive mood, and invited Margery to dinner. He took her (to use his expression) to a posh restaurant. Towards the end of the meal he asked her whether she was going to the White House. 'I go there as seldom as I can,' she said.

'You still love David?'

'I prefer not to discuss that.'

As they emerged from the restaurant he suggested she come to his flat. Nicole didn't exist yet. She said she was going back to the hotel where she was staying the night. She spoke distantly, as though there were no bond between them. 'It wouldn't be the first time, my lovely one,' he said.

'As I don't need a thousand francs there won't be a second time,' she said, and walked away.

The cheek of it, he thought.

Remembering it, fury shook him as if they were still in the street outside that restaurant. He should have run after her, grabbed her by the waist and said, 'I'm the only good cock you ever had, you pute de Pigalle.' As the aircraft touched down in Nice he admitted that at the time he wouldn't have dared to say that since he was in the pay of Mme Hermine and herself. Admitting that proved that the fit was over.

He smelt the scented air, thought of Shaftesbury Avenue

172

and Nicole's yellow belly, and decided to have a jolly good time, leaving his mission for the following morning. He had been to Monte Carlo several years ago, naturally without Nicole, and had won a few thousand francs in the Casino Municipal. Wouldn't it be nice to repeat the performance? With his hold-all that contained the necessities for one night he boarded a bus to the Principality. If I were rich I'd live here, he said, standing outside the Hôtel de Paris, and nearly had another fit because he possessed no wealth. On his way to the casino he wondered what had become of David after he had lost both his wife and his seat. He couldn't have got far since he never saw his name in the newspapers. Had he his fortune he would have a large villa in Monty, and spend his nights in the casinos of the Riviera, have no wife, keep no mistress, but pick up a different dazzling girl whenever the fancy took him, which in his case would be twice a day. This climate makes me randy, he said half-aloud.

He entered the casino all smiles. 'Never saw such a fat man looking so happy,' said one thin old Englishwoman disapprovingly to another. Then they both gasped because it was rouge that turned up and not noir.

When Walter went to the bar he was still all smiles. He had won over five hundred francs, which would pay for the fun he had in mind. Among the ancient regulars of the Casino Municipal he noticed a slim girl with auburn hair, not difficult since she was the only young person in the crowd. She was drinking tomato juice, that is to say she just stood in front of it at the counter, now and then taking a little sip. She wants to make it last, thought Walter. She won't be expensive. He ordered half a bottle of champagne. The girl smiled at him. 'Do you understand English, mamzelle?' he asked.

'Sure,' she said. 'I'm South African.'

'A lovely country,' said Walter who had never been there.

'If it was such a lovely country I wouldn't live in Europe.'

Not a good beginning, he said to himself. 'Drink up that red stuff, and have a glass of champagne.'

'Now you're talking,' she said. 'Kate's my name. What's yours?'

'Walter.'

'Cheers, Walter,' she said, lifting her glass.

She accompanied him back to the gaming table. He got numbers 14–17 à cheval, and when the croupier pushed his winnings to him she took fifty francs which made him raise his eyebrows. She explained she was playing for him because it was her lucky day. She put them on number 26, and number 26 won. She said they would divide the winnings. When she had lost her half she asked for the other half. 'After all it was I who put it on 26,' she said.

'Listen, Kate. I'm not a beginner, got me? You took the fifty francs from me, it was superbly generous of me to let you keep half of the winnings. If you lost them it's your funeral. I don't like being taken for a fool.'

'You mean, fat hog,' said Kate, and walked away.

I'll look for a girl outside, said Walter to himself. They're all corrupt in here.

He left the casino six hundred francs up, not to be sniffed at, though he regretted having lost back most of his winnings with horrible Kate.

He dined well, looked around for some skirt, but somehow he couldn't find any. He returned to the casino, not to play, only to have another look round. Not a single woman took his fancy. Eventually he saw one standing behind an old man seated at a gaming table. He smiled, she smiled back, he tried out his French on her, she understood he wished to offer her champagne, and taking his arm she led him to the bar. To show her she was dealing with a man of substance he ordered a whole bottle of champagne. Before the girl could lift her glass Kate appeared, whispered into her ear, the girl gave Walter a cold glance, said, 'Pardon,' and went off with Kate. Walter emptied the bottle, and because he was furious he emptied it swiftly. He returned to the roulette table, and when he left the casino he had just enough money left for a cheap hotel, breakfast, but no lunch. Luckily he had his return fare to London.

He slept in a decrepit hotel in Nice, and in his dream he saw Nicole as she had been in her attractive days. As he got into bed with her, Kate appeared and pulled Nicole away. He woke up at dawn, and had another fit of anger, Margery again, but this time the Margery who had calmly informed him that, having made their fill and because doing the same over too long a period can become dangerous, she and Mme Hermine were getting out of the business.

'And what will I do?' Walter asked pathetically.

'That's strictly your affair,' Margery said.

Victor came the next day to say he also was through. Walter didn't dare to remonstrate with him as Victor invariably helped him out in gratitude for his never breathing a word to anybody about his true relations with the White House, Margery and Claud.

Recovering fron his fit he thought of the two thousand pounds Victor had promised to leave him, and being Victor he had kept his word. Telling Claud the truth wouldn't be an unfriendly action to Victor : it would be to have his own back on that bitch of a Lil, and on bloody Margery too, two birds with the same stone.

At half past eight he was in Cannes, ready for the task. He rang Margery's number, she answered sleepily and harshly. Walter had the knack of imitating voices. The one he chose was of a school mate of his who had committed suicide before male homosexuality became legal.

'Am I speaking to Mrs Darnell, Claud Darnell's mother?'

'You are. What do you want?'

'My dear Mrs Darnell, could you be a perfect angel and call Claud to the phone?'

'He isn't here. He's staying in the Hôtel Romei. You'll find the number in the book.'

'Hôtel Romei? Is that the right way to pronounce it?'

'It is.'

'You're perfectly sweet. I can't thank you enough.'

Margery had rung off after saying, 'It is.'

Mme Romei smiled at the fat man, and asked if he wanted a room.

'Monsieur Claud Darnell, madame.' He pointed at the house telephone.

'I'll ring up to his room,' said Mme Romei. 'I know he's up.' She knew that because Modeste had come down already. 'Here, monsieur.' She handed Walter the receiver.

'Claud,' said Walter, who found it difficult to speak in his normal voice, 'this is your father's old friend Walter Elking speaking. Remember me?'

'Very much so. You're in Cannes?'

'Only for a few hours. Could we have breakfast together?'

'I'll be down in five minutes.'

Mme Romei beamed on Walter and wished, as she wished several times each day, that she spoke English. 'Friend?' she asked.

'Mon bon ami,' said Walter.

A client came to speak to her. When she had finished with him Claud was in the hall.

'Here I am,' said Claud. 'The breakfast-room is over there.'

'We can't talk here,' said Walter as they went in. 'They're unmistakably English and American. Is there some café nearby?'

'Come across the street,' said Claud, who had no more cause to fear going into the breakfast-writing-room : Rudge had left in high dudgeon the day before, Mme Romei's doing.

The café, where David regularly breakfasted, was still empty owing to the (for Cannes) early hour. Walter and Claud sat down at a table near the door, and Claud smiled at Walter, waiting to hear what his father's old friend had to say.

'Do you think they give you bacon and eggs?' asked Walter.

'I'm sure they do,' said Claud, waving to the waiter. 'I only have coffee and a croissant.'

'I carry the English climate with me,' laughed Walter.

As you couldn't know how the young man would react, Walter wolfed down the bacon and eggs before coming to the point.

'Claud, I was devoted to Victor. I can't say the same about your mother and Lil.'

'I'm devoted to Lil.'

'She has a shady past.'

'That's no concern of mine,' said Claud, flushing with anger. 'She's been like a mother to me.'

Forget Lil for the moment, Walter warned himself. 'I'm on a business trip in the South of France. I decided to look you up because there is something you must know. It's in your interest to know it.'

What could it be? Claud wondered. Surely Ludmilla hadn't sent him.

'Tell me,' he said, then lifted his cup. 'Too hot.'

'It'll be a shock to you, but you'll derive immense benefit from it. When you think it over you'll be grateful to me. You were brought up on a lie. Victor isn't your father. David Woodlow, an enormously rich man is your father. When Margery carried you he paid Victor to marry her so that you should be born in wedlock. His wee trouble was that he was married. The White House was given to Victor by your real father as part of the bargain. The farm too.' To do his duty by Victor Walter added, 'Being a perfect gentleman Victor kept his side of the bargain.' He blinked, Claud was staring at him, his mouth open, no light in his eyes. 'Did you get me?' Claud continued to stare. 'Did you grasp what I was saying? You're not Victor's son.'

Claud rose from the table. 'You lie,' he said. 'You're a liar. I'm my father's son. Go. Anyway, I'm going. My father wasn't a liar. He wasn't like you. Go.'

Claud steadied himself, then rushed from the café.

Walter finished Claud's coffee, feeling mighty pleased with himself. He could picture Lil's and Margery's faces when Claud told them that he knew. Claud had invited him to breakfast, so let Claud bloody well pay for it. In any case he had put him on the right track. Claud could take now as much money as he wanted from David who hadn't bothered to add a line when he sent him the fiver after his release from prison.

'Monsieur is coming back,' he said to the waiter, then left the café. He would take the first bus to Nice to board the first aeroplane to Heathrow.

'Who's that?' called David. The strenuous knock on the

door had jerked him out of sleep.

'It's Claud, sir. I must see you at once.'

'Enter.' He took in Claud's white cheeks and the darkness in his eyes. 'Anything wrong with Modeste?'

'Answer me,' cried Claud. 'Was my father my father? Or are you my father?'

'What are you saying?' asked David to gain time. 'Close the shutters, please. The sun blinds me.'

'Are you my father?'

'What nonsense.' That also was to gain time. 'I don't know what you're talking about. I won't say a word more before you close the shutters.'

Victor had taught Claud manners, and David smiled as the young man went to close the shutters. Had Margery spilled the beans? Was it to unite the three of them at last? Victor was dead, so no impediment was left. The notion of it moved him as he hadn't imagined he could be moved again. All repaired, the shutters closed, but the window opened to let in the fresh air of truth the three of them needed. It was miraculous. Claud came back.

'Don't think I'm mad,' he said. 'I'm very fond of you, sir, so I can insist on the truth. I'll go mad if my father isn't my father.'

'Look here, Claud,' said David gently, 'I can't answer you if you don't explain. Is my father my father? Melodramas are for the stage, not for hotel bedrooms at this unearthly hour.'

'I'm sorry, but you can't guess what I feel. My father was my ideal, there was nobody I admired more. I'd rather die than not be his son.'

'For God's sake, boy, tell me what it's about.'

'A man my father knew, his name is Walter Elking . . .'

'I used to know him.' So it wasn't Margery. That changed everything.

' . . . came here, oh just half an hour ago, and told me that my father wasn't my father. He said that mother was your mistress, and when she was carrying me you paid my father to marry her because you were already married.' That swine

178

of a Walter should get his facts right, thought David. 'Because of that money my father had to pretend that I was his son. That's what that man said. So my father was a beastly crook, a man who lied to me all my life, to me who loved him so ... forgive me.'

Claud burst into tears, his whole body shaking. He raised his hands to his eyes to cry into them, and repeated between sobs, 'Forgive me, forgive me. I shouldn't.'

David got off the bed, pulled Claud's hands down, and as Claud cried out, 'Who's my father?' David said, 'Victor Darnell. Everything that man said to you was a wicked lie. But what else can you expect from an ex-jailbird? Don't give it another thought, Claud.'

'And all that about you giving my father money?'

'Why should I give your father money?'

'He said you gave him the White House.'

'Never in my life. He bought it from me and the only reason I didn't tell you that it was once mine was because I forgot it ages ago. Seldom went near it.'

'Oh, I'm glad, you don't know how glad I am. I'd have died if only one word of it were true.'

'Not a word of it, Claud. Your father was an honourable man, and,' he couldn't resist adding, 'no bogus parent, however hard he tried to play the part could inspire the filial love you felt for your father. Now go to the bathroom, wash your face, then go to Modeste.'

'I'll be grateful to you all my life,' gushed Claud.

'Because I told you the truth?'

'Because you saved me. Isn't it marvellous that I could come from that horror straight to you? But why did he pick on you?'

'Because he never liked me, and wanted to make mischief. Anyway, forget it. Don't tell your mother because it would only upset her. Go and wash your face.'

'I know I'm too young to suggest it,' said Claud when he came out of the bathroom, 'but may I call you David?'

'Call me David, dear boy,' said David, surprised by the catch in his voice.

'How lucky you were at hand, David,' said Claud, grinning happily.

When the door had closed on him David went into the bathroom, and looked at himself in the glass. He couldn't help winking at his reflection. A latter-day Pagliaccio. A narrow shave, he added.

He arrived in Margery's flat earlier than was his habit.

'Madame is in her bath,' said Sylvie.

'I'll wait. How's your health?'

'I'm in a very poor way.'

'So are we all.'

'I won't live much longer. I'll tell her you're here.'

He poured pastis into a tall glass, added ice and water, and as he raised the glass to his lips Margery came into the room, looking far from pleased.

'Some awful queer woke me up this morning,' she complained. 'He rang me to get Claud's address.'

'Walter Elking,' said David, 'could imitate voices perfectly. He used to keep Victor and me in fits of laughter imitating the colonel's or the RSM's voice.'

'What has Walter to do with it?'

'He was the queer who rang you up. He saw Claud, and told him that I was his father.'

'Why did Walter do that? I bet he fell out with Lil. Give me a pastis. I bet too that he wanted to sleep with her and she refused. How did you find out?'

'Claud came straight to me.'

'What did you say to him?' she asked, lying back on the sofa.

'I said Walter was a damned liar, and Victor was his father.'

'So you kept up the lie. What an unnatural father you are.'

'A thoughtful father, Margery. Had I told him the truth it would have killed him.'

'But he'd have known that you were his real father.'

'The boy loved and admired Victor. The truth would have been the end of all he believed in, it would have wrecked his life. He burst into tears while he waited for my answer.'

'One thing is certain : it wouldn't wreck his life if he found out that I'd worked in Pigalle. I wonder why he didn't tell him that too.'

'You don't go to a person whose confidence you want to gain, and compromise yourself, too,' said David. 'If Walter had said that he'd worked with Victor in the white slave traffic, it wouldn't have inspired Claud to believe a word he said, I mean doubt that Victor was his father.'

'Where's Walter? Give me another pastis.'

'No idea,' said David, going to the table. 'I hope for his sake he doesn't run into Claud again. By the way, I told Claud not to say a word about it to you.'

'I wouldn't have let you down if that's what you're afraid of. I kept my trap closed from the start, and it'll remain closed as long as you want it.'

'Margery,' sighed David, 'another few bricks have been added to the wall that stands between us.'

'Le déjeuner est servi,' said Sylvie from the door, wincing with pain.

'She said she would die soon,' said David on their way to the dining-room.

'She'll outlive us all,' said Margery. 'You'll be pleased to hear that I asked fat Mme Romei, her niece and Claud to dinner. You'll come of course.'

'My dear Margery, frankly I can't. My little scene with Claud took more out of me than I expected.'

'Poor Papa David,' she laughed.

2

When she was alone, Elfrida's lunch consisted of an egg on toast and as much Corsican wine as she could drink, a potent wine that sent her to her siesta with flushed cheeks. The air conditioning of the block of flats invariably went wrong when the warm weather came. It was insufferably hot in her small flat, as if the drawn Venetian blinds spat flames. There were two looking-glasses in the bedroom, both reflecting her shape while she undressed. She was pleased with the body of the desirable ripe woman they showed. Yet David didn't want it.

She returned to the sitting-room, where she had lunched, poured out another glass of wine and drank it in one gulp. Then she went back to the bedroom, the looking-glasses reassuring her that her figure was still desirably ripe. She lay down, her hand travelled down her body, her legs opened as she closed her eyes. When the climax came she cried out, 'David, I love you,' then turned on her side, and fell asleep. The real fun began. She and David lay side by side on a little beach closed in by palm trees, the mountains behind them. David smoked a cigarette, gazing at the sky. She wore a two-piece swimming suit, the sun shone on her navel, and she took off the top part of the swimming suit. David continued gazing at the sky. She pulled off the lower part unnoticed by David who had finished his cigarette and was burying the stub in the sand.

'David,' she said in a hoarse voice.

He looked at her, uttered a cry, then threw himself on her. She woke up, shaking all over. Her finger finished what the dream had left unfulfilled.

She rose depressed, feeling as though she had emptied a whole barrel of Corsican wine. She was sweating, heaviness weighed her down, it was an effort to take herself to the bath-room to have a shower. A little refreshed, she dressed with great care, for she would soon be in David's presence. She tidied the sitting-room (the charwoman came only in the mornings), then made her bed. Every time she left her flat she left it with the hope of bringing David back. David should never see the bed unmade, the plates and glasses un-washed. When it was all spick and span she rang down to the porter, asking him to get her a cab. A last look in the glass, then she departed with undying hope in her heart. The cab was at the door.

The first person her eyes beheld was David seated at their usual table, a bottle of wine in front of him. They were true wine drinkers both of them. Yet if he chose pastis or whisky she took the same, for she drank whatever he drank. He didn't look too happy. What could ail her darling?

'Here I am, David,' she said, sitting down.

'Want some of this tavel?'

'Yes, please. Where's Margery? Shouldn't she be down?'

'She has Claud and his future wife and aunt-in-law for dinner, so she probably won't come down.'

'Are we invited?' How soothing the we sounded.

'I said I wasn't going.'

'In that case I'm not going either, David.'

He nodded before drinking more wine.

'Who's that man?' Elfrida asked. 'He's smiling at you.'

David looked up : a tall bearded man had come into the bar. Despite his beard David recognised him : Alec Wrightson, the Liberal, who had beaten him at the 1951 General Elections. He lost the seat at the next one. Wrightson was on his way to the table, his hand outstretched.

'My dear Woodlow,' he said, 'I recognised you at once.'

'Same here,' said David, rising. 'Have a drink.' He introduced Wrightson to Elfrida.

'Meeting after all these years,' said Wrightson, sitting down. 'I'm indeed glad to see you again. Nobody could have a more chivalrous opponent than you were. I retain the happiest memories of our little battle.'

Balls, said David to himself. I was chivalrous because my heart wasn't in it any more. 'You're being too kind. Are you in Cannes for long?'

'Passing through on my way home. Given up politics. Haven't you, too?' David nodded. 'I'm in the City.'

'It's either the House or the City. With that beard I thought you couldn't be in the City.'

'Beards are the fashion. I walked past here, saw London Bar, so came in for a couple of drinks. What are you doing, Woodlow? I mean when you're in England?'

'As I live here I do nothing in England. Here even less.'

Wrightson began to talk of the 1951 General Elections, of his defeating David with a majority of only six, and David saw himself dragged back to Jessica's grave, Brinworth Hall ringing with emptiness, and his state of mind at the time. Too much, he said to himself as he rose.

'It was grand seeing you, but Mrs Formby and I have an appointment at the other end of Cannes.'

Elfrida stood up like one in a dream, in fact in the dream she had during her siesta. She had to control herself, otherwise she would have taken David's arm.

'It was wonderful seeing you,' said Wrightson. 'Made my day, the best memory I'll take back from the Riviera.'

'How everybody loves you,' gushed Elfrida as they came out into the street.

'I could have wrung his neck, poor fellow. He loves remembering what I prefer to forget.'

'You look upset, poor David.'

'No longer.' He looked up and down the street. 'Where do you want to go?'

'Anywhere you want to, David.'

'Let's take a taxi and go to Nice. What I need is a real, big town.'

'I love Nice,' said Elfrida, who seldom ever went there.

It was sheer bliss sitting so close to him in the taxi.

'That Mr Wrightson seemed to worship you, David.'

'Forget Mr Wrightson,' he nearly snapped. 'Not a period I care to remember.'

It must have been the year when his wife died, my poor David, she said to herself. If she saw someone who reminded her of her years with the late Mr Formby, would that upset her? It couldn't, since she had forgotten him and their time together. Anyway, he would be over eighty now, a frightening thought. She wriggled a little closer to David. Her scent he found too strong.

'Do you think,' she asked, 'that Claud will be happy with the French girl?'

'I'm sure he will. She's an awfully nice girl.'

'If I had a son I'd insist on his marrying an English girl. Same world, same habits.'

'But you haven't a son.'

'True enough,' she sighed. 'Are we going to the Promenade des Anglais?'

'To the old town.'

'I don't know it.'

She irritated him while they strolled in the old town, no sense of the past, no feeling for the picturesque. It gave him an almost sadistic pleasure to take her into mean bistrots, make her drink vin ordinaire, and rub shoulders with unsavoury looking people. He had to admit she was game, doing all she could to please him.

'I'm getting tiddly,' she giggled as they came out of the seventh bistrot.

'Let's go and dine,' he said. He had no wish or desire to go to Alice's London Bar. Margery was sure to bring down her guests. I don't want to see either Margery or Claud tonight, he said to himself.

'What did you say?' asked Elfrida.

'I said let's go and dine.'

'But didn't you say something afterwards?'

He shook his head: his thoughts were too loud. Damn Walter for stirring it up, damn Margery for not understanding him, rot poor Wrightson for bringing back the past.

He took her to a restaurant filled with repatriated settlers from Algeria, a noisy set of people, not the sort Elfrida cared for. However, there was a large looking-glass on the wall opposite, and smiling at their reflection she found herself and David a well-matched pair. The couscous she didn't enjoy, yet ate it with pretended gusto to please David. She could spend her life dedicated to pleasing her man. They drank plenty of Côte de Provence, then had armagnac.

I'm coldly drunk, thought David on leaving the restaurant, Elfrida was happily tipsy. 'We must look for a taxi to take us back,' he said.

'Oh, David, could you come for a nightcap to my little flat? I'd love you to come.'

He glanced at his wrist watch: not even eleven. 'All right, Elfrida.'

'Oh, David,' she murmured.

In the taxi she wondered whether he would let her take his hand. She looked at him from the corner of her eye: he was lighting a cigarette. After taking the first puff his right hand dropped on his knee. Slowly her hand approached it, then thanks to the courage the wine she had drunk gave her she grabbed it, murmuring again, 'Oh, David.' He pressed hers, pure bliss, but then he withdrew it. Never mind he had pressed it. She moved her leg, it touched his, more than bliss. 'How I love sitting here with you, David,' she breathed.

'I'd a most annoying day,' he said, crossing his legs.

'Because of Mr Wrightson?'

'Plenty of other reasons. One side of me calls it nonsense, the other has a different word for it.'

'I do know that feeling, know it only too well.'

Stupid fool, he thought. 'But both sides badly need a drink,' he laughed.

'I've all the drinks you can ask for,' she said. 'Look how pretty the moon is.'

'It has a contract with the travel agents, that's why it shines every night.'

'How wonderfully witty you are. I could listen to you day and night.'

'I don't feel witty a bit.'

'You can't help being clever, witty and amusing even if you don't feel like it.'

'Poor girl, if you believe that.'

He had called her girl, which meant that she was his girl. She took his hand again, this time he didn't pull it away. Why not? he thought. Anything to snap him out of his present mood. He wished he hadn't said a word to Margery. He should have let Walter remain the unknown queer on the other end of the line. Stupid Elfrida's hand was clammy.

'Here we are,' she said when the taxi stopped.

In the lift she stood close to him, smiling coyly. Reaching the flat she asked him to sit down in the sitting-room and choose any drink he wanted while she put on something lighter.

'Any wine? I need wine tonight.'

'I have only Corsican.'

'Let it be Corsican.'

She fetched two bottles from the kitchen, then, saying she

wouldn't be long, she went to the bedroom, leaving the door ajar. From where he sat he could see her in one of the glasses if he leaned forward. Men always leaned forward. She switched on every light. However, David sat back, looked round the room. Though he had lived for donkey's years in a hotel he hadn't lost his taste for good furniture and interior decoration. Soulless and without any personality, was his verdict.

Elfrida had a transparent summer dress with which she had to wear a petticoat. As she changed into it she wilfully forgot the petticoat. Moreover, she took off her bra before putting on the dress. Thus everything showed. She lifted her arms, and when they were high enough the dark red nipples came into evidence. The pubic hairs were a small wood with brown autumn leaves. She scented herself, then entered the sitting-room, where too she switched on all the lights.

'The light is too strong,' said David.

'I like strong lights,' she said, lifting her arms.

He looked up, and saw it all. Not too bad, he thought, for one who wished to forget. She saw that he saw, and her happiness was complete.

'Give me your glass,' she said, leaning over him, the scent enveloping him. 'We'll feel like a couple of Corsicans with this wine.'

'Napoleon and Laetitia,' David couldn't help saying.

As she had no idea who the Corsican's mother was she gave him a huge smile before filling the two glasses. She pulled up a highbacked chair, sat down on it, and in the harsh light she could just as well have sat down naked.

'How do you like my dress?' she asked. 'So comfortable.'

'I don't see why you wear it at all,' he said, putting his hand on her thigh. It was a bit hefty, but the skin was soft.

'Do you really want me to take it off, David?' she whispered modestly.

'I really want it,' he said, his hand travelling up the thigh.

'David,' she cried, shaking, 'I'll take it off, but first go higher . . . oh, I love you, I always loved you.'

She let out a shriek, then threw herself on him. He found

himself in a cloud of scent filled with flesh. She kissed him with such strength that he lost his breath. Her arms held him hard. 'David,' she panted, 'I love you, David. Come straight to the bedroom, my beautiful David.'

When he reached the bedroom she was on the bed already, lying as she had lain before her siesta. He looked at her with some amazement. Since he had come to live in France he had made love only with girls of Nelly's type, here today, gone tomorrow, and no personal relations. Now in front of him was a woman, offering herself because she loved him, so she said. It was an experience he had chased away long ago. For a moment he was moved despite the large dark red nipples, too large breasts and hips.

'I waited for this for years,' she said.

He undressed, and she watched him undressing as you watch the unveiling of a statue by a great sculptor. When he got on the bed she pulled him to her, and on penetrating her he was surprised by her vehemence. Not since his time with Margery had he felt a woman reacting like that. If only it were Margery, but even if they tried it again it could never be the same. Elfrida was mostly soft flesh, whereas Margery had been elegant bones. Elfrida was on the peak of delirious bliss.

'I knew it would be good,' she panted, 'but I never hoped it could be so perfect.'

'Don't flatter me,' he said to be kind. 'It'll go to my head.'

'If I tell you all I feel about you . . .'

'You mustn't. I'll go and get a drink.'

'I want a drink, too.'

'I'll fetch it.'

When he came back with two glasses of wine he looked at her still sprawling on the bed, her eyes aglow with contentment. Frankly, not my cup of tea, he said to himself, not even my soup tureen.

'What makes you laugh, my darling David?' she asked.

'The memory of this pleasant evening, Elfrida.'

'We must have many more such evenings, David,' she said a little frightened.

'My dear girl, you must consider this just a little episode in our lives.'

'Aren't I good in bed?'

'You're perfection itself, but you must understand that I can't enter into a regular affair.'

'Because you're in love with Margery?' she asked, sitting up.

'Our relationship is on a very different level. It's simply because of my nature and temperament. I lost the gift of loving.' He kissed her on the forehead. 'My dear Elfrida, I'm immensely grateful to you. You helped me to kill an awful day. Now, as the saying goes, I'll love you and leave you.'

He dressed quickly with his back to her, without even glancing at his reflection in the glass, for if he looked into it he would see her. He turned round when he had put on his jacket, and there she was, straight behind him, still naked, large tears streaming down her cheeks. The best policy was to ignore the tears.

'See you tomorrow afternoon,' he said, 'and we'll go on where we left off when we came into this room.'

'As you like, David,' she sobbed. 'Don't forget that it was the greatest moment of my life.'

'You're sweet,' he said, patting her wet cheek.

'I thought in my stupid way,' she said in a small voice, accompanying him to the door, 'that tonight broke down the barrier you always put up. Nevertheless, it was wonderful. I could spend the rest of my life sitting at your feet, gazing up at you like a faithful dog.'

'It wouldn't be worth it. Besides, it's out of the question. Thank you again.'

He thanked me, she howled as the door closed on him, as one says thank you after a tea party.

Tomorrow he would send her a huge bunch of roses, he said to himself going down in the lift. On second thoughts he decided against. The poor creature might misinterpret his gesture.

It wouldn't hurt him to go on foot to the Hôtel Romei. The later he lay down, the more easily he would fall asleep.

The moon lit up the mountain-range and the flat sea. There was too much of Elfrida, and that went as much for her sentiments as for her body. Imagine having a proper affair with her, overwhelming would be an understatement. She had said she wanted to sit at his feet, naked of course, and if he rose she would trip him over to protect him from the outside world. In time she would see to their changing roles. Overwhelming women carried iron rods hidden inside their loving bodies.

He found the night porter asleep as usual. He gave him a shake.

'A Mme Darnell has telephoned an hour ago,' said the night porter, rubbing his eyes. 'She asked you to go to her however late you arrive.'

'I'm going at once,' David said.

Had Walter been to see her?

'At what time did M. Darnell come back?'

'At eleven with Mlle Modeste.'

It was three o'clock : he just couldn't make it out.

He saw Nelly through the open door of the all-night café. Why hadn't he thought of her before going to Elfrida? Simpler and lighter. Still, he had no cause to fear Elfrida. He had made it plain to her, if necessary he would make it plainer.

Alice's London Bar was closed. He went up the stairs to Margery's flat. The door flew open almost before he rang the bell. Margery stood there, wearing a dressing gown.

'Sylvie is dead,' she said.

'Poor Sylvie, how sad,' he exclaimed.

'Poor Sylvie, how sad,' she mimicked. 'The only time I really need you, you decide not to be in the bar. Come in, don't stand gawping in the doorway.'

'When did she die?' he asked, following her to the drawing-room.

'Shortly after Claud and the Romeis left. I went to the kitchen to have a word with her. She sat at the table, I spoke to her, no answer, no movement. I became frightened, touched her shoulder, she fell forward, her head banging the table top. "Sylvie, Sylvie," I hollered. I must have wakened up everybody in the house. I flew down to fetch you . . .'

'Terribly sorry.'

' . . . you weren't there. Alfred came up. "Elle est bien morte," he said. I phoned my doctor. He came at once, said she was dead, surely a heart attack. Do you want to see her?'

They went to the guest room. On the bed lay Sylvie, taller in death than in life, her hands folded, her rosary wound round them, a taper on each of the bedside tables. Margery burst into tears.

'Do you know what it means to lose somebody who has shared your life?'

'I do, Margery.'

She turned away from the bed, dried her eyes with the palm of her hand, then said, 'If you ever do the dirty on me by dying I'll be unconsolable.'

He took her hand and kissed it.

3

Light June rain fell on the White House, the garden and the fields, and standing at the window of her bedroom Lil thought it was fitting weather for her departure. If the sky knew what she felt the rain would be harder.

'Want any help, miss?' asked Jones, the gardener, from the other side of the bedroom door.

'Take down the two suitcases if you want to,' she said, opening the door.

'This will be a very different place without you,' said Jones. 'How many years?'

'I prefer not to count them.'

'What about that book there?'

'It belongs to the library. I'll take it down myself.'

'Don't leave, miss, without saying goodbye to the wife.'

'Of course not. Where's Wilf?'

'Out in the rain.'

'Don't forget to lock him up after I've left.'

'We'll take him to the cottage, and bring him back when Mr Claud arrives. Then he'll start looking for you.'

'I'll miss him, don't you worry.'

'I'll take these to the porch,' said Jones.

Lil sat down on the bed to read for the tenth time the letter she was leaving for Claud. He had rung up three days ago to announce his and his wife's arrival. Claud married but not to Ludmilla. God was her witness how many times she had tried to argue with Victor: 'With a girl like Ludmilla, Claud would never be happy.' Victor's invariable answer had been that in marriage you didn't look for happiness: you looked for peace. 'Can there be peace without happiness?' she asked. He said it was important to distinguish between the two, and since she was an ordinary woman with little education she stopped arguing. Was the letter badly written? She read it, her lips moving, wishing that Victor were there to correct it.

'My dear little Claud,

'When your father died I told you I was going to go away because there was no need left for me here. I was, as you know, your father's invention, he made me and I was what he made me. With him gone to the Heaven he believed in I have no place here any more. I stayed on only to leave you the house as it was in your father's time. I am going today.

'You, my dear little Claud, I loved you as if you was my son. I will always love you as if you was my son, but from far. You now have a wife, you said on the phone how happy she made you. I leave you to her, and all God's blessings. You know how easily you catch cold. So be careful with it. Keep as good a suvenir of me as I keep a suvenir of you, my dear little Claud.

'Lil'

She would leave the letter on the hall table.

She looked round the room for the last time, thinking of the nights, waiting till Claud had gone to bed before going to Victor. Then of the last two years when he let her come to his bedroom no longer. Well, if that helped him to Heaven she had no right to complain, in fact it was her duty to rejoice. She had seen Father Turle from a distance the other day. She couldn't help turning back. Yet she didn't curse him, for which Victor was surely grateful to her.

She closed the door, then went down to Victor's bedroom on the first floor. The windows had been opened by Mrs Jones who, to show that she had arrived, opened all the windows in the house in summer as in winter. Lil sat down on Victor's bed. A tractor made an infernal racket. There had never been anybody like him. One day, singing his praise to Miss Hulbert, the old bawd observed that he was no better than she. Lil nearly flew at her. 'You don't deserve to kiss his feet,' she said. 'It's not what you do, but who you are. He did what he did for the White House, for his boy. He wouldn't have done it just to grab and grab like you.' Oh my great Victor, she said, looking up at the Crucifix hanging above the bed, if you could make a woman as happy as you made me there can be only greatness in you. And the way you loved and brought up Claud. And this house. What it was like when I came, and how lovely it is now. She heard the telephone bell. Let Mrs Jones take the call, it was no concern of hers any more.

'Miss,' shrieked Mrs Jones, 'where are you? A call for you.'

'Coming,' she called, opening the door.

She threw a kiss at the bed, and going down the stairs she called herself a fool for not asking Mrs Jones to tell the caller that she had left already.

'Hullo,' she said.

'Hullo, Lil. This is Walter.'

'What do you want?'

'I was just wondering what's becoming of all of you. Any news from Marge or Claud?'

'They're perfectly well, but it's no business of yours.'

'Nothing unpleasant? No trouble?'

'None whatever. Why should there be?'

'I said I was just wondering,' said Walter in a disappointed voice.

'Stop wondering because I'm ringing off. You got your two thousand pounds so we don't want to hear any more from you.'

She put down the receiver, thinking it was clever of her not to say she was leaving. He wouldn't dare to come near the White House after his performance last time. She went to the kitchen, where the Joneses were having their elevenses.

'As I told you,' Lil said, 'Mr Claud is arriving with his wife late this afternoon. Mr Ringham will be coming in to see them, but please be here too. Mr Claud told me on the phone that his wife understands a little English, but I don't think she understands Sussex.' The Joneses laughed goodhumouredly. 'So speak to her very slowly. Mr Claud says she's a very good cook.'

'Snails and frogs,' said Jones.

'Snails, frogs, or bats,' said Lil, 'you be as nice to her as you can. That girl will be out of her element, so you make her feel at home.'

'Mr Claud will be with her,' said Mrs Jones, 'and she looks real lovely, not like a certain Miss Coke we know.'

'How do you know she looks lovely?' Jones asked his wife.

'Miss showed me the snap Mr Claud sent her.'

'Can I see it?' asked Jones.

Lil took the snapshot from her bag. Jones agreed that she looked lovely.

'But why couldn't you wait to see her?' asked Mrs Jones.

'Because I must go. Now goodbye both of you. All the best.'

'We come to the door,' they said. The doorbell rang. 'The taxi.'

Wilf had been busy at the other end of the garden, but when he heard the taxi he ran up, barking. He saw Lil come out of the house, accompanied by the Joneses. He jumped up on her, and she stroked his golden head, murmuring, 'Don't forget me, Wilf,' then got into the taxi. Jones closed the door quickly so that Wilf shouldn't jump in. The drizzle turned into a shower as the taxi went out through the gate.

'You said Folkestone, not Dover,' said the driver.

'Folkestone Cemetery,' said Lil.

It was pouring hard when she entered the cemetry. A burial was in progress only a few yards from Victor's grave, the ceremony conducted by Father Turle. As she came nearer, the mourners thought she belonged to their group. Father Turle was sprinkling Holy Water on the coffin, Lil stopped beside Victor's grave. A mourner made a sign to her, she had no idea why, yet she diffidently approached the open grave. She was given the sprinkler, an old man gently pushed her forward, and she sprinkled the coffin, blushing hard. As she lifted her head Father Turle's eyes met hers. For the first time she found them kindly eyes.

'We all meet up in the Bull and Goat,' the old man whispered.

The little group left the graveside, Lil in their midst. A hand touched her arm : it was the priest's. 'You want to stop here, don't you?' he said, pointing at Victor's tomb, standing between her and the mourners, who thus were forced to move on, leaving Lil behind.

'I hear you're going away, Miss Cowling,' Father Turle said. She nodded. 'I wish you well and hope you'll find peace and happiness. I'll pray for you.' Lil nodded again, afraid if she spoke she would burst into tears. Father Turle bowed, and went off to find the mourners, several umbrellas close to each other in the rain.

Who was that person on whose coffin she had sprinkled Holy Water? she wondered in the train taking her to Charing Cross. A man, a woman, old or young? She would never know. Victor had said that we were all equals in the eyes of God. Remembering those words it gave her a sense of comfort that she would never know who the dead person had been.

At Charing Cross she took a taxi to Streatham, where her cousin May lived above her greengrocer's shop. Lil asked the driver to take her suitcases into the shop and leave them in a corner. May was a childless widow, short, with a pleasant face and gay eyes. She was three years older than Lil, but from childhood onward she had obeyed and admired her. Her late husband had made life difficult for May because of his constant gloom. She was behind the counter, talking to the assistant, a red-haired girl with a moon face.

'You look after the shop,' May said to the girl. 'We're going upstairs for a mo'. You take one suitcase, Lil, I'll take the other.'

The small flat smelt of floor polish.

'So here you are, Lil. I'm real glad to see you. I'll make some tea. First tell me what your plans are. You're still lovely to look at. I don't think you have to plan long ahead.'

When Lil had worked for Miss Hulbert she had told May she was living with a man who kept her. To say she was a call girl might have shocked May.

'No more men for me,' Lil said, sitting down in the armchair in front of the television set. 'Nobody could replace him.'

'All widows say that,' laughed May. 'I'm the only exception.'

'It's true in my case probably because I'm not a widow, only a slave that refused and still refuses freedom.'

'What will you do?'

'One of the many things I learnt while I lived with him was cooking. I learned to cook well because he loved good food. I'll put an advertisement into *The Times*, saying experienced cook willing to cook for lunch or dinner parties, and you'll see the number of answers I get.'

May looked disappointedly at her idol.

4

David idly watched Blandine dressing. He had picked her up in a bar in the rue d'Antibes, a tall, dark-haired girl who faintly resembled Margery. She said to him when she was dressed, 'I'm going straight back to my husband.'

'I can't imagine you with a husband,' said David just to say something.

'I can't either,' she smiled, 'but he does exist. Good night, mon chéri. Don't forget my little present.'

He held out a hundred-franc note, she put it into her bag, gave him a ravishing smile, then left. David lit a cigarette.

He had kept his distance from Elfrida, not difficult since it was easy to fall back into his normal routine. For a few days she had tried with imploring glances to remind him of the night of her bliss. The glances were ignored. He took great care not to be alone with her. Funny that she hadn't turned up tonight in the bar and afterwards in Margery's flat. 'Perhaps she has found a man at last,' said Margery. David wished from the bottom of his heart that she had.

Lying back in the armchair he asked himself what Elfrida had expected from him. A long liaison? To live together? The very idea of living with her filled him with nausea that turned almost into panic as he pictured life with her. Listening to her eager, empty chat would drive him crackers, to have that opulent body at his beck and call would kill all sexual desire in him. Anyway, there was no danger of that ever happening.

He would go on taking to bed girls like Blandine, or Nelly who had disappeared from the all-night café, which meant he wouldn't see her again. If Blandine gave up visiting the bar in the rue d'Antibes he wouldn't see her again either. Blandine had mentioned that she had a husband. Probably some complicated story was attached to it, a story he wouldn't hear thanks to their limited relationship. If you knew a person's story you were in a way attached to that person. No attachments for him. His attachment to Margery was enough for a lifetime. She had a new lover, a Danish sculptor with the smile of a little boy. How long would it last? That was strictly her affair.

How pleasant it was to be alone, tied to nobody. In his hotel bedroom he was the master of his existence. He could go to bed when he wanted, get up when he felt like it, and then organise his day as it pleased him. If his faith in Margery hadn't failed him on that Saturday in the rue des Capucines they would be living together, and he would love every minute. They were made for each other, perhaps the reason why fate kept them apart. As he wasn't living with her, living alone remained the only possible alternative. He wished it weren't so hot in the bedroom.

The summer season was in full swing, turning Cannes into the secondary residence of every second Parisian. He vaguely thought of leaving Cannes for a couple of months, well aware that he couldn't summon the energy to make a move. Besides, he would be away from Margery.

He was pleased that Claud had returned to England, for he had become too fond of him, and there had been some dark and weak moments when he wanted to blurt out the truth. Luckily he remembered in time Claud's anguished eyes after his meeting with Walter. Victor must remain the father. It was better, therefore, to keep his distance from Claud, too. Claud had asked him to stay with him and Modeste when he came to England. Since he had no intention of going to England it was easy to promise that he would.

Claud and Modeste were married in Notre-Dame-de-Bon-Voyage, Margery smiling during the ceremony as if she couldn't stop smiling. Mme Romei wiped her eyes. The newly-weds spent their honeymoon in Piedmont, where Modeste had distant relations. They returned to Cannes, and after three days in the hotel they set out for the White House, taking Marie-Bénédicte with them. David and Mme Romei saw them off at Cannes railway station; Margery was too busy in Alice's London Bar to go to the station.

'Won't it be too miserable for Modeste?' asked Mme Romei on the way back.

'What do you mean?'

'I mean the English fog.'

'The sun of the Midi will shine through it. Trust Modeste for that.'

'You say such nice things,' sighed Mme Romei.

David undressed, went to the bathroom, then took himself to bed. Now this is what I call peace, he thought switching off the light.

He slept well, no nightmare disturbed him. He woke up soon after eight, and as it was too early to get up, he turned on his side, closing his eyes. He found himself addressing a vast crowd with Jessica at his side, her eyes encouraging him. He could hear his voice, the crowd couldn't, and the louder he shouted the more the crowd seemed to get impatient because of his silence.

'The telephone,' said Jessica, lifting the receiver.

David awoke, frowned at the telephone, 'Who dares to ring me so early?' he yelled at it before answering.

'Who's that?'

'Elfrida. David, I'm pregnant. We're going to have a baby.'

David's laughter shook the telephone wire. The birds that sat on it flew off in haste.